finally,

forever

Also by Katie Kacvinsky

First Comes Love
Second Chance
Awaken
Middle Ground

Dedicated to

Ryan

Thanks for providing the real-life inspiration that helped
write the ending of this book

finally,
forever

by
Katie Kacvinsky

PART ONE: THE ROUTE

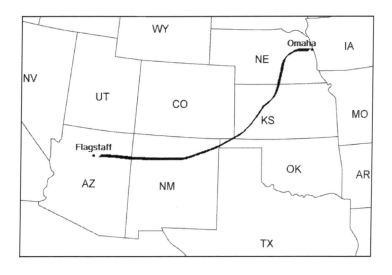

~ Fifteen months after the break-up ~

Gray

I'm leaning against the side of my car in a parking lot in Omaha, Nebraska, and I'm watching a girl. White smoke curls around the open hood of her station wagon, and I can only make out a skinny leg and a faded, gray tennis shoe.

The sun bakes on the blacktop between us and I swear the ground is so hot it has a pulse. I've been outside an entire thirty seconds and my forehead is already drenched in sweat. I can feel it beading on my neck and sliding down my back like a tiny fingertip tracing my spine. It's the kind of humid heat that touches everything, even the thickest spots of shade, and it's too heavy and stubborn for a gust of wind to blow.

She takes one step back and I notice a baggy blue skirt stick to her knees in the stagnant air. The rest of her body is lost inside a white cloud. I slowly walk towards her to see if she needs help.

She tries to wave the blanket of smoke out of her face with a long, skinny arm, as wiry as a tree limb. She takes another step back and her face comes into view. I freeze. I melt.

Oh. My. God. It couldn't be.

I stare at her like she's haunting me. Maybe I'm hallucinating. What is Dylan doing in Omaha, Nebraska of all places? She coughs and takes another step back and manages to smear engine grease across the side of her face. There's no doubt that it's her. She's the same, all six feet of her long, lanky body. The only difference is her hair is cut short, tied back in two, messy pigtails that barely graze the top of her shoulders.

She glances around the parking lot, her eyes passing over me at first and then they focus and then they hold and expand to twice their normal size. Her mouth falls open like she's staring at an apparition. I wonder if I am, if I'm dreaming up this entire scenario. Maybe I fell asleep at the wheel. Maybe any second I'll collide head-on with an eighteen-wheel semi truck. I would almost prefer that nightmare to this reality.

I spent the last year trying to purge every memory of Dylan from my mind. It was a Dylan Detox. I listened to *Anna Begins*, by Counting Crows, and let the melancholy verses nurse me back to emotional health. It's nice to know somebody out there understands. Music can save you from yourself. It's like a friend whispering, *Hey, it's alright. I've been there. I got through it and so will you.* It's my self-prescribed medication for post relationship therapy. I convinced myself those song lyrics carried into my own life, my own situation with Dylan, and it all was starting to make sense. It helped me to move on.

But Anna doesn't come back at the end of that song. She doesn't suddenly reappear at a road stop in Middle America and say 'Hey, remember me?'

What do I do now? Adam Duritz, where are your song lyrics for this prophetic situation?

I used to hope that one day I would run into Dylan again, but Hope can be a dangerous demon disguised as an angel. Hope works alongside Fate and Luck and Timing, and they're all co-founders of the conspiracy group I like to call Team Asshole.

We both stand there, facing each other like we're statues glued to the asphalt parking lot. I hear car engines moan to life and tires peel away and I wonder if I died and went to hell. What do you do when you run into the ex-love-of-your-life? Say hello? Hug? Shake hands? Run for your life? I'm afraid to open my mouth. I might scream.

Dylan smiles, this elated, glowing smile as if our chance meeting should be serenaded with a marching band and fireworks.

"Gray? What are you doing here?" she asks me, as if I'm the one that's out of place in this picture. Her voice knocks me back to reality and I have to take a side step or I'll fall over. It's amazing how just the sound of a voice can make your entire stomach cramp and your head spin and your heart convulse in one simultaneous jerk.

"I played ball out here this summer," I say, a little roughly.

"Oh," she says and nods. "Was it a summer sports camp?"

I almost laugh at her question. "Summer sports camp? Otherwise known as minor league baseball," I clarify for her. Her knowledge of sports is up there with my knowledge of cosmetics. I cross my arms over my chest, displaying the muscles that I've worked on building for the last three years, as if to back up my statement.

"What are *you* doing here?" I demand.

For a tiny, split second I get the crazy feeling Dylan followed me here because she desperately missed me. She showed up to surprise me at a roadway oasis to confess she can't live without me, that if she graphed all the happiest times in her life, all of her peaks exist because of *me*. Her indifferent shrug dismisses this idea.

"I was on the highway until Orson decided to crap out," she explains and points to the open hood. I walk up to her latest beater-mobile. Where did she get this car, a junkyard? The station wagon looks like the one my grandparents used to drive that we called the 'grocery-getter,' complete with wood paneling along the sides. I stop a few feet away from Dylan, careful to give us some distance. The engine is still steaming.

I look inside at the fried motor that's expelling fumes of burnt oil, and back at her. I know her too well to sympathize with this situation. One thing obviously hasn't changed.

"What is it with you and owning piece of shit cars?" I ask her, looking into her eyes.

"Ssh," she says and covers her lips with one finger. She rubs the fender like she's stroking an animal's head. "He can hear you." She looks down at the singed engine with concern. "Someone has to love him," she says.

"Cars aren't dogs, Dylan," I inform her. "They don't have abandonment issues."

She just blinks back at me like she never considered this.

"They're meant to be *safe* and *reliable*," I state, two words that probably don't exist in her vocabulary.

Dylan smiles and lifts the bottom of her white t-shirt to wipe off sweat dripping down her forehead. I can't help but notice her bare stomach and it gives me a momentary brain lapse. Her skin has always had that affect on me. A fifteen-month separation might erase some feelings, even memories, but you can never erase that unstable, uncontrollable, unexplained phenomenon called attraction.

"I always thought interior lighting was the most important car feature," she tells me. "Ambiance is critical. This one has red interior lights. It's like Christmas every day."

I look at her messy pigtails.

"When did you chop off your hair?" I ask, since the last time I saw her, it fell halfway down her back.

She grabs a pigtail between her fingers and examines the choppy end of it. "After you White-Fanged me in Albuquerque," she says.

I lean in close enough to see the blue, brown and green swirls that swim in her eyes. Her eyes meet mine and a chill runs down my back, even in the sauna-like heat of the late summer day.

"After I what?" I ask and a voice interrupts us, calling out my name. I spin around and Rachel is standing on the curb next to the restaurant entrace, regarding each of us with interest. She adjusts the yellow cardigan open over her navy blue sundress. Her light brown hair is parted on the side and pulled back in a low ponytail.

"There you are. They seated us inside," she says to me. She looks curiously at Dylan who is looking at her and they both turn and look at me. I connect an awkward triangle of stares. Behind Rachel is the entrance to The Palm Tree Cafe. I'm still wondering who decided to name a restaurant in Omaha after a tree that would never naturally grow here.

"Rachel, this is Dylan," I say as she walks up to us.

Dylan reaches out her dirty hand. Her long, skinny fingers look like they were soaked in black grease. Rachel extends her own clean, small, manicured one. If hands express any sign of personality characteristics, these two are complete opposite. Dylan grabs Rachel's hand in a firm hold and gives it one solid pump, her signature shake. Rachel takes her hand away and examines the track of gray fingerprints pressed on her skin like stamps. She rubs her hands together and studies Dylan.

"How do you two know each other?" Rachel asks.

"We…," my voice trails off because our past is as easy to summarize as the plotline to a TV drama. I look at Dylan for help and she takes care of making the introductions.

"I met Gray in Phoenix a few years ago," she explains. "We're old friends. My car just died, and I'm trying to get to Flagstaff."

"Flagstaff?" Rachel says and my heart pinches in my chest. Oh, no. Don't say it.

"Well, Gray's on his way back to Phoenix today."
She turns to me and smiles like she solved all of our
problems—not started them. "You can give her a ride."

I clear my throat, trying to loosen a knot of
tightening nerves.

"Oh, no, that's okay. We, no…," Dylan blunders
and then she stalls and looks at me to gauge my reaction.
I have to remind myself to breath. A shallow stream of
hot hair squeezes through my throat. I swear I'm having
a panic attack.

"I'm sure there's a bus," Dylan offers, and I nod
enthusiastically. Yes, a bus, or a plane, or a hot air
balloon, or she can roller skate there for all I care. That
girl is not getting inside my car. It's my one safe place.
It's my zone of tranquility.

"Seriously," Rachel encourages us. "You can split
gas money and trade off driving shifts. It's perfect." She
gives me a confident nod. "We'd feel better knowing
you were driving with someone," she tells me.

I laugh, a sort of choking sound. It brings my voice
back.

"Why are you going to Arizona?" I demand to
Dylan.

Her constant smile flattens at the corners. "There's
a family emergency," she says. She studies my eyes, the
hostility behind them, and understands what I'm not
saying. "But don't worry about it. I don't want to
inconvenience you."

"That's just silly," Rachel pipes in. I want to
smother my hand over her mouth. Don't you see you're
planting the seeds of misery by inviting this girl back
into my life?

"I *could* use a ride," Dylan says.

Rachel nods. "Isn't it great how fate makes everything work out?"

"It is strangely fortuitous," Dylan agrees and meets my eyes for a second before I look away. I pretend to be fascinated by a red minivan pulling into the parking lot.

"What are you going to do with your car?" Rachel asks.

"Well, it's not actually *my* car," Dylan says. I just named it. "It's Nick's."

Just as she says this, a guy is walking up behind her, holding two sweating bottles of water and smiling.

"Making friends already?" he asks and offers her a bottle. He gives her this adoring grin and it makes the muscles in my arms tense.

I stare him up and down. He's exactly my height, 6'3". His brown, wavy hair is pulled off of his face with a pair of sunglasses. He has these large, brown, really friendly eyes. He looks outdoorsy, dressed in a blue polo shirt and tan cargo shorts. I'm a good judge of character and Nick seems, unfortunately, cool. I automatically despise him.

Dylan turns and makes the introductions. As soon as she says my name, Nick's eyes dart to mine like a javelin, hitting me with an unbelieving stare. I meet his gaze and hold. We're having some kind of stare-down and I'm determined not to look away first. He definitely recognizes my name. I wonder how much Dylan told him about me. I wonder how badly he wants to kick my ass right now. But he doesn't look angry, or jealous. More than anything, he looks curious. He actually reaches out his hand to shake mine. I grab his fingers and try not to squeeze so hard I break one.

"Gray. Nice to meet you." He says my name like he's referencing a famous book title and I almost smile at his lie. He shakes Rachel's hand and regards both of us for a few seconds like he's trying to piece something together.

"I'm Dylan's boyfriend," he says, specifically to me. He throws an arm around Dylan's shoulder just to be a jackass. Even Dylan looks surprised by the possessive gesture.

I fight to keep my feet steady. I've seen one other guy touch Dylan in my life. Once. And I threw a baseball at him as hard as I could. The same territorial instinct is flooding back.

"I found a red eye flight I can catch tonight," he says to Dylan and leans in closely to tell her. Their noses almost touch. "Are you sure you want to take a bus to Flagstaff?" he asks her. "I found some cheap flights to Phoenix."

Dylan points over at me and grins like I'm her old pal from the neighborhood and this isn't at all weird.

"Funny, actually," she says. "Gray's headed to Phoenix today. So, he can drop me off in Flagstaff."

"Wow," Nick says and he regards me again. "What a coincidence."

Tell me how you really feel.

"I wish I could go with you," Nick says and coos into her shoulder.

"Why don't you guys eat dinner with us first?" Rachel offers. "Before you head out?"

I stare at Rachel. Aren't you just full of fun ideas?

"Perfect," Nick agrees. He reaches down for Dylan's hand and I'm already stalking towards the front entrance. I have to make a concerted effort not to stomp. I hear Dylan commenting on the name of the restaurant behind me, and she wonders out loud if palm trees grow in Nebraska. If I weren't currently loathing my life, I would smile.

Dylan

I watch Gray disappear inside the restaurant so fast it's as if he has a jet pack strapped to his back. I can almost see a trail of steam shooting out behind him. I stand in his exhaust trail, stunned.

"Dylan?" A voice calls out to me through an abyss of shock. "Dylan?"

I blink and Nick's worried eyes come into view.

"You're scaring me. Focus," he says and shakes my shoulders until I meet his brown eyes. "I'm worried you're going to lose control of all bodily functions right now."

Fragmented words start to appear in my mind but they're not forming sentences. They drift and float but they're difficult to connect. My heart is pounding as if I just sprinted around a track. Only one thing is clear.

"He hates me," I say.

"Hate can easily be confused with love," Nick argues. "They're very similar emotions if you think about it."

Now I'm even more confused. "That makes no sense, Nick."

"Love never does," he says. "We'll figure it out. I promise."

"I can't believe Rachel offered Gray to drive me. It was *her* idea. Shouldn't she be a little wary, loaning out her boyfriend to chauffer random girls across the country?"

Nick rests a hand sympathetically on my shoulder. "Honey, have you looked in the mirror recently? I don't really think she was intimidated. You have a huge smear of motor oil running up the side of your face. And under your chin. And how did you get tire tread marks on your t-shirt?" He shakes his head and makes a "tsk, tsk," sound.

"But, you told Gray you're—"

"Just play along right now," he interrupts. "Trust me."

He swings the glass door open and half shoves, half escorts me inside the restaurant. My skin immediately chills in the freezing blast of air conditioning. The room is as cold as a meat locker. I bypass the hostess stand and head straight for the restroom sign. My thoughts are racing in front of me and I'm picturing Rachel's face. One word: Rebound. She's not right for him. She has a limp handshake that lacked any assertiveness. Her brown eyes are dull and lack any spirit of adventure. And she wears cardigans. In the summer.

I push through the door and stand in the middle of the room.

She would probably keep his cupboards stocked with daily multivitamins, one for men and one for women. She'd make cut-out cookies for his games, in baseball shapes and frosted with his number. She'd pack picnics with napkins neatly wrapped around the silverware. Her meals would contain the appropriate number of servings from the food pyramid.

But Gray doesn't want to be taken care of, he wants to be challenged. Doesn't he? Or what if all the things that I think make her wrong for Gray are all the things that make her right? And why is a wide set man wearing a greasy apron giving me the stink eye? What is he doing in a women's restroom?

"You lost?" he asks me and I blink a few times.

"I just need to use the bathroom," I say.

"Does this look like a bathroom?"

I glance around at the industrial sized ovens and grills and refrigerators and I can smell sausage cooking and I can hear the bubbling sounds of French fries cooking in the fryer. Two other cooks, both guys, turn and stare at me. I see lots of piercings and tattoos and I get the feeling I've stumbled into a motorcycle gang's initiation meeting. And they're not happy about it.

I slowly take a step backwards.

"Sorry," I say and try to redeem myself. "My nose must have been lured inside by the incredible smells." They look me over.

"Did you get hit by a car?" one of them asks.

"No."

"Run over?" another inquires. "Did you hit your head?"

"No. Why are you asking me that?"

"You have tire tread marks all over your shirt," the heavier cook says, pointing at me with his spatula.

"And you were mumbling to yourself when you walked in," another adds.

I press my hands over my hips. "Look, if you want to know the truth, it feels like I have been hit by a car, okay? I just ran into the ex-love-of-my-life in the parking lot outside, looking like this," I say and open my arms wide. "He hates me, and he happens to have a beautiful, freshly-showered trophy girlfriend. So can you give me break?"

Their faces fill with understanding.

"You want a slice of bacon?" the cook asks.

"Yes!" I cry. One of the guys pushes a folding chair in my direction and I slump down and press my hands over my face.

***

Ten minutes and two crispy slices of bacon later, I find my way to the bathroom. I walk inside and use a paper towel to scrub the grease off of my face and hands. It refuses to abandon the beds of my fingernails. They're black around the cuticles and under the tips. It's a dirt tip manicure. Lovely.

I look at myself in the mirror. My pigtails are a mess. One actually looks longer than the other. Sweaty bands of brown hair have escaped and cling to my neck. I do my best to wipe them away. Pools of freckles stand out on my face like tiny pebbles, darkened and multiplied by the summer sunshine. I look down at my stained t-shirt. There's no point trying to wipe away the tread marks.

It's no wonder Rachel offered to let Gray drive me to Flagstaff. Nick's right, she isn't intimidated. I literally look like I have been run over by a car.

I lift my chin and stare into my eyes. They glow, amber and blue and green under the fluorescent lights. My eyes have never been able to settle on one color. I always loved Gray's eyes because they're so piercing blue, so constant, so different from mine.

I mutter two words out loud.

"Fuck it."

I've never cared what anyone has thought of me before. Why start now? I don't see limitations. I see opportunities. It's my superhero power. Captain Optimist.

I turn and walk out of the bathroom. My self-esteem gives self-doubt a flying ninja kick out of my head and I start to smile. I spot their table in the corner of the restaurant. Gray and Rachel are sitting across from Nick, and another older couple is sitting at the table. I pull back an empty chair next to Nick, across from Gray.

"Where were you?" Nick asks as I sit down.

"In the bathroom," I say. "Well, first I took a quick tour of the kitchen. Did you know they have a walk-in cooler, the size of a bedroom, just for pies?"

They all stare at me, but I ignore the disbelief in their eyes.

"The cooks are really nice guys," I continue. "Brock, Gus and Steve. Two of them are brothers and one of them builds motorcycles. He works here to supplement his income until his business takes off. Oh, and they say that the bacon scrambler is the house specialty. It's not on the menu—you have to ask for it. The locals call it The Cardiac Arrest."

Everyone is still staring at me.

I raise my filthy hands. "What?"

The woman next to me introduces herself as Rachel's mom, and her father is sitting next to Rachel on the other side of the table. I shake their hands and I'm already assessing the lunch predicament.

Parents? A send off dinner with her parents? This is beyond a summer romance. First comes a family-infused goodbye. Next comes the engagement announcement.

I glance at Gray and a memory snaps on in my mind. After a birthday party when I was little, my favorite helium balloon slipped out of my fingers and floated away in the sky. I screamed and cried helplessly as I watched it go. It was my first experience with loss. My mom was calm and consoled me and told me there were hundreds more like it. She told me I might even find one I love more, waiting somewhere for me to discover it. She told me, "Let it go, Dylan." I always remembered that story because I've used it before in my life when I'm letting go of a place, or a person that I love. But looking across the table at Gray, I'm starting to lose faith in that fable. Experience is a valuable messenger of truth. There aren't a hundred more people like Gray. Maybe what my mom should have said was, "Dylan, the next time you love something, hold on tight."

Nick takes my hand and examines my fingers.

"Couldn't get the grease out?"

"I hear the grunge look is in," I say and my hand slips out of his. I pick up the menu and open it like I'm opening a treasure map. Emotional drama is an excellent appetite stimulant. I'm starving.

"You'll love this menu," Nick says. "Breakfast is served all day."

"As it should be," I say.

The waitress comes by to take our orders and Rachel is showing Gray some photos on her phone. He's leaning close and they're smiling and laughing at some inside joke and I hate sitting here. It's like sitting bare naked under a hot sun, feeling your skin burn.

I watch Rachel's eyes and when they aren't staring into her phone they're focused adoringly on Gray. Just like he deserves. Maybe she isn't a rebound. Maybe he finally found his constant sun.

Nick nudges my arm and the waitress is waiting for my order. I order a grilled cheese sandwich and curly fries. Gray and Rachel's dad order the bacon scrambler. Rachel asks for a garden salad with dressing on the side. I try not to gape. Who orders a salad at a greasy spoon diner? Another huge strike against her. I wait for Gray to state the same fact, but he just ignores her ordering misdemeanor.

Rachel explains my situation to her parents and they nod and seem concerned and relieved.

I glance across the table at Gray a few times while everyone's talking. His eyes never once meet mine, as if he's immune to my presence. Or highly allergic. He's mostly staring at the white, paper table covering. He's changed over the past year. His arms are more muscular and defined. His chest is broader and thicker and fills out his t-shirt. Any boyish looks Gray had before have vanished. His hair is the shortest it's ever been, almost buzzed. All the curls are gone. It's thick and dark and he's as tan as teak wood and his blue eyes stand out, like two pools of sky. I wonder if his hair is still long enough to run my fingers through. Wait, scratch that. I wonder if it's long enough for Rachel to run her fingers through. Gagh.

I look from Rachel to Gray and jealousy kicks at my heart. She must wear pointy high heels because her kicks are sharp and they hurt. But my mind fights back. Have they listened to every single Ryan Adams' album in the dark? Have they dissected the seven voices of a harmonica (depressed, angry, happy, exited, withdrawn, reminiscent, melodramatic and heartbroken)? Highly doubtful.

Gray slips into quiet mode. A 'closed' sign snaps on over the door of his mouth and when he's like this, he's doing one thing: thinking. I'm curious to know what he's thinking about.

Nick takes charge of asking questions and most of them are directed at Rachel.

"What did you do this summer?" he asks her.

"I had an internship with the baseball team. I want to go into sports journalism," she says and starts discussing baseball team statistics over the summer. She actually sounds like a sideline news reporter.

Blah, blah, sports talk. I love watching sports but talking about them is about as exciting as listening to someone list the contents of their refrigerator. My eyes wander and I notice a cup of children's crayons in the middle of the table. I grab the cup and color on the paper tablecloth.

Without realizing it, I draw a cactus, a green saguaro like the one Gray and I used to take pictures of in Phoenix. I have an entire album dedicated to the strong personalities of saguaros.

I look up at Gray and he notices what I've drawn and for the first time since he's seen me, he meets my eyes and smiles. It's one of his signature slow smiles. It's like a big thaw, and my entire body heats up in response. I feel my mouth drop open and my heart knock against my ribs. All the old feelings rush back. One familiar smile can do that, it's like a zipper loosening you up, opening you, spilling out all the old feelings you neatly folded and packed away.

I tune back into the conversation when Nick touches my hand.

"Dylan?" he says, "Channel 2, please."

From the confused stares that pass around the table, I explain that my brain is like a remote control, always surfing the channels.

"Nick is Channel 2," I say. "When he wants my attention he switches me back."

Rachel and her parents smile at our inside joke but when I look at Gray he's glaring at Nick.

"What do you do, Dylan?" I look over at Rachel-the-Rebound's mom and think about her question. What do I do? Saying I take pictures is so prosaic. It doesn't touch on what a photograph captures, on the compelling story inside every shot. So, I explain it the best I can.

"I build bridges," I say.

"What?" The entire table says at the same time. Except for Gray. His mouth is tight.

"You build bridges?" Rachel repeats. "You're a construction worker?" she asks and I shake my head at her literal translation. Doesn't she have any imagination?

"Architecture?" Rachel's mom guesses and I love this game.

"Closer," I say.

"She's a photographer," Gray says.

"It's a lot like building a bridge," I point out. "You know, it connects people to other places. It brings us closer. It allows us to see places we never had access to before."

Nick smiles and rubs his fingers over my hand.

Rachel's mom grins. "Where did you go to school?"

"UT," I tell her and she asks if that's the University of Texas. I shake my head.

"The University of Traveling," I say. "It's a wonderful academy." Nick laughs next to me.

"She's self taught." Gray translates my words into normal conversation. I'm a little disappointed.

"She's brilliant," Nick says. "She just sold an entire stock of photos to a children's book illustrator. They've already hired her for another job."

"Dylan, that's an unusual name for a girl," Rachel's mom comments.

"I was named after Bob Dylan," I say with a shrug. "My parents were hippies."

"What?" Gray says. "You never told me that," he insists. His voice is mixed with admiration and disgust.

"If I was a boy they were going to name me Bob," I say and shudder. "I much prefer Dylan. I'm not a fan of monosyllabic names ending and beginning with the letter B."

"Are there any other than Bob?" Gray asks me.
"I hope not," I say.

Gray

The waitress walks up to our table holding six dishes in her outstretched arms. It's an impressive balancing act. She slides a plate in front of me, piled with hash browns, eggs, sprinkled with salt, dressed in ketchup, marinated in grease and splattered with orange droplets of cheese. And the crowning glory: six slices of bacon crisscrossed over the top. My mouth starts to water.

I glance at Dylan and she's staring at my plate with jealousy. Our eyes meet and we have a telepathic conversation.

Thanks for the recommendation, I say with my eyes.

It's beautiful, her wide eyes say back.

I nod slowly. *I know. Have you ever seen such amazing food display?*

She shakes her head. *It looks like art.*

Worthy of a museum exhibit, I nod.

Can I try it? Her eyes are pleading.

I shake my head. *No way.*

Her eyebrows crease. *Please?*

I narrow my eyes. *You should have ordered it when you had the chance. I can't make your choices for you.* My eyes cut over to Nick and back at her. *Your loss.*

Just one bite?

I sigh and scoop up a spoonful of scrambler onto my fork and drop it on the edge of her plate.

"Thanks," she says and grins but I don't return the smile. I lean my shoulder into Rachel's.

"You want in on this?" I ask her and point to my meal. She looks between my plate and her dad's and grimaces.

"I'm not into heart attacks," she says. "No thanks."

I pop a slice of bacon into my mouth and shrug. My heart has already been stomped on, kicked, and sewn over. It probably resembles the shape of a something really pathetic, like a giant teardrop. A little bacon grease isn't going to do any damage that Dylan hasn't already inflicted.

"Nick, what do you do?" Rachel's mom inquires. I look at him and assume, if he's friends with Dylan, he's going to invent a metaphorical job description like, "I produce oxygen and help the world to grow and photosynthesize," when really, he does landscaping.

"I'm in my second year of vet school," Nick boasts. I glare at him. In Dylan's dog-obsessed world, that means he's a superhero.

"Wow, that's a fascinating field," Rachel's mom says.

I stare down at my plate. Yeah, fascinating. I bet he's all the fun and spontaneity of a medical textbook.

Nick smiles and studies his hand with this sweeping motion and for a split second I think he's gay. Wow. My brain is reaching for anything to wish this guy out of Dylan's life. More specifically, out of her pants.

"That's how Dylan and I met," Nick says. His eyes look whimsical for a second, recalling the magic moment that Dylan appeared in his life. "I was interning at an animal shelter," he begins, "And Dylan was there, volunteering." He rubs his hand over her shoulder. "I took one look at her, holding a pug like it was her own baby, and I knew she was the one. I had just finished assisting on an emergency surgery for a golden retriever puppy that was hit by a car. We saved his life."

Rachel's mom presses her hand over her heart and gives Nick this adoring smile, like he's some kind of messiah.

I look over at Nick. One word: Tool. He's mister wanna-be-outdoorsy, but he's just a textbook nerd. Vet students are like doctors. They have one routine in their schedule: Studying at the nerdatorium and then eating at the nerdery with all their fellow nerdites.

"Well, what an interesting lunch," Rachel's mom says. "Eating with a veterinarian and a professional photographer and a professional baseball player." Nick perks up at this. I feel his eyes on me.

"You play pro ball?" he asks. He looks impressed. Are you intimidated, Dr. Boy? Afraid muscles might be sexier than degrees?

I take a bite of my hash browns. "Minors," I clarify. I don't really want to talk about baseball. I don't want to talk, period. I want to get the hell out of this situation.

Nick unrolls the paper napkin and sets it on his lap. Did he seriously just put a paper napkin on his lap? I'm calculating all of his movements, storing them away so I can overanalyze them later, and rip him to shreds in my mind.

"This summer was the best team we ever had," Rachel's dad brags. "Won the conference. Gray got MVP."

"I had a great team around me," I say.

"You worked harder than anybody," her dad argues. "The Dodgers noticed."

"You signed?" Nick asks me.

I shake my head. "We're still negotiating," I say. "I'll probably play one more year in college."

"It must be a lot of traveling, a career like that," Nick says.

I narrow my eyes and wonder what he's implying. "It will be," I say.

"You won't live in one place for very long?" he assumes.

"It depends," I say. "In the minors you can get bumped around a lot."

"And there are 162 games in the season," he informs me as if I don't know the schedule. "Only certain people can handle that kind of lifestyle."

I stare him down, wondering why he cares.

"It's perfect if you're a baseball fan," Rachel chimes in and leans her shoulder into mine. I look at her and smile, thankful I have a fan in the room.

The waitress hands us our check and she looks out at the window at the hazy sky.

"Ya'll drive safe," she says. "Storms are on the radar."

I look at the waitress and raise my eyebrows. Literally or figuratively? I want to ask.

Dylan

I follow Nick out of the restaurant into the scorching heat of the parking lot, soaking up the sun's rays like a sponge. Gray and Rachel are still inside, saying goodbye to her parents. We stop next to Orson.

"Why did I have to run into him, Nick?" I look up at the sky like I'm asking a higher power. "Why did this have to happen? Why?"

"Dylan, you of all people know that life never happens the way you expect it to. Shit happens, and how you deal with it—that's life."

I sigh. "I can't believe you told him you're my boyfriend."

He gives me a devious smile. "Was I convincing?"

"Convincing?" I say. "That performance was Oscar worthy. Definitely deserving of a Golden Globe award. At the very least, a nomination for best actor in a drama from the Screen Actors Guild."

He smiles at my sweeping compliments.

"It was too fun," he says. "That boy gets even hotter when he's angry. I can totally see how he's amazing in bed. All that passion? Yum."

"Since when do you know anything about baseball?" I ask.

He takes off his sunglasses and wipes them clean with his shirt. "My dad's dragged me to Milwaukee Brewers games since I was eight. We had seats right behind the home plate. It was great ass viewing—made me want to get to home plate if you know what I'm saying." Nick laughs and slides his glasses back on over his forehead to keep the hair out of his eyes. "Poor man, if only my dad knew what I actually used my baseball glove for."

I cringe at the thought but then Nick points behind me and I turn to see Rachel and Gray walking outside. They stall at the front doors to say goodbye and I look away so I don't have to see Gray touch her.

"Listen to me," Nick says and turns my shoulders back to him. I feel like my bones have turned as malleable as rubber. I want to slump to the ground. "She's not right for him. He's not in love with her."

"How do you know?" I ask.

"Guess who he spent all his time watching over dinner?"

I shake my head. "He hardly ever looked at me, Nick. He was avoiding me."

"Exactly, because he was too busy glaring at me. Which I didn't mind, he has gorgeous eyes, even when they're plotting my death. You could see a landslide of jealousy streaming down the kid's face."

I look down at the ground. "I can't lie to him."

"You don't have to. I did the lying for you. It's what friends do."

I watch Rachel get into the driver's seat of a bright blue hatchback. As she drives away I catch sight of her personalized license plate and my mouth drops open. It says HORSES.

Horses? I try to envision Gray living on a horse ranch. Equestrian gear, wranglers, chaps? He hates country music (unless it's alt-country, he claims). Even my wildest imagination can't visualize it. She is so wrong for him. What is the girl version of a tool? An accessory? Yes! That's what she is. A safe, simple accessory.

I remind myself to breathe. Jealousy is toxic. It's unattractive. It's like poison in my brain, and even worse, it's a waste of time. I extract every bad thought I have of Rachel and I put them in a glass jar in my mind. I tighten a lid around the jar and toss it over my shoulder. I feel a little better. I'm determined not to think another negative thought about Rachel. I'm determined not to think about her, period.

"Are you sure you'll be okay if I leave now?" I ask Nick.

He nods and looks longingly at his car.

"I'll stay with Orson until the end," he says and rubs the hood of his car. "He deserves that much."

I stroke Nick's cheek. "He's had a good life," I say. "This wasn't your fault. It was just his time," I say.

Nick inhales a sharp breath and nods. He squeezes his eyes shut as if he's trying to block out a painful image. "I wish I understood. Why Orson? He was such a great car. He never got in an accident. He never even got a flat tire."

I grab his hands in mine.

"Because somewhere, up in heaven, an angel needed a car. The strongest, most reliable car, and God looked down on Earth and searched for the perfect, German made vehicle that was safe enough for his angel to drive. And he chose Orson."

Nick nods.

"Now, whenever you see a shooting star at night, you'll know it's an angel driving Orson through the sky."

"That was so beautiful," he says. He looks over at the sidewalk and Gray steps away from Rachel and turns to us. Nick tightens his fingers around mine.

"I bet you'll be in each other's pants in forty eight hours."

"That's not what I want," I say. "I just want Gray to be happy."

"Exactly. That's why you need to do this." He grabs my arms and pulls me close. "Kiss me like I'm Gray."

Before I can respond he scoops up my face in his hands and leans down and kisses me full on the lips. Nick's lips are huge and wet and smother me. It's more like a face wash than a kiss and I can't pull away because he's holding my head in his hands so tightly I can feel each of his fingertips dig into my scalp. I try not to gag on his tongue.

He lets go and gazes lovingly into my eyes.

"I love you, Dilly Bar," he says to me.

Now I don't have to lie, because I love Nick.

"I love you a billion times a gazillion," I say and I turn around to see Gray standing a few feet away, looking sick to his stomach, like he just stepped in a fresh pile of vomit on the sidewalk.

Gray

I feel vomit creeping up the back of my throat and I swallow it down. *Dilly bar?*

Dylan tells me she has to grab a few things from the front seat. Nick pulls her duffel bag out of the trunk, the huge one she brought to New Mexico last spring. I walk over to my trunk and open it up and shove a few baseball bats to the side to make room. Nick hands me the duffel bag, a sleeping bag and a pillow.

"You know, Dylan's mentioned you before," he says.

"Is that right?" I ask as I try to maneuver my crap with Dylan's crap so all of our crap is together again, entwined under the same roof. Crap.

"You two used to date."

Date. That's a funny word to describe the path of emotional chaos that constituted our failed relationship. I give her luggage an unnecessarily hard shove.

"Something like that." I look back at Nick and he's watching me. Is this is another staring contest? I always win.

"She tells me everything, you know."

I slam the trunk closed and narrow my eyes.

"Everything?" I ask. Like how once I got her off eight times in one day? How I probably hold an orgasm world record? What have you got, Dr. Boy? I blow out a sigh and tell him what he already knows.

"Then you know you can trust her," I say. He narrows his eyes and nods slowly.

"Take care of my girl," he says and turns and walks away.

I get in the car and shut the door a little too forcefully. Dylan sits down in the seat and closes the door and I can't help myself.

"Did I hear him right?" I ask, and look over at her. "*Dilly bar*? Seriously, he calls you Dilly Bar?"

"What's wrong with it?"

"What's wrong with it? Want to get out a pen and paper while I list all the things that are wrong with it? You have a great name. Why does he need to mutilate it?"

"It's a nickname," Dylan defends him.

"Oh," I say and start the ignition. "So, what do you call him? S-Nick-er bar?"

It wasn't the conversation-ending comeback I was hoping for because Dylan laughs out loud, this blasting laugh that comes all the way from her stomach. My lips tighten because it's one of those contagious laughs that make you want to join in and I refuse to give her the satisfaction of thinking I'm enjoying this quality time together.

"It's better than horses," Dylan mumbles and clips her seatbelt into the lock. I ask her what she means.

"Your girlfriend's personalized license plate? Horses?" Dylan says.

What is she talking about? My girlfriend? I swore off relationships over a year ago, just like I gave up pot. They both are equally bad for my health. But I know what car she's referring to.

"Rachel?" I ask.

Dylan nods. "You know, I try really hard never to judge people Gray. I've always left the judging up to you. You're a natural at it."

"Thanks," I say.

"And I'm not jealous," she points out. "I'm just, a little disappointed."

I can't believe this. "What, you can date somebody and I can't?"

"It's not that. She just isn't what I expected. I know you're really picky about who you let into your life and—" she cuts herself off. Dylan is terrible at verbal insults. It's one of her best qualities.

"Go on," I say.

"No, I don't want to be mean. She's very nice. She has very clean fingernails and I respect that." She frowns at her own abused nail beds.

"No, please, I really want to know what you're thinking," I say, fascinated.

Dylan sighs. "She just isn't interesting. At all. I'm sorry, I know it's a terrible thing to say. But it's the truth."

I pinch the inside of my cheeks between my teeth to hide my smile. Dylan looks genuinely upset and there is something extremely satisfying about her expression.

"You've known her for an entire hour."

"You can tell within five minutes if a person is interesting," Dylan argues. "Actually, I've mastered figuring it out in one minute by examining shoes, hands, fingers, eyes and chosen mode of transportation."

"What are you, a forensics investigator?" I ask and she ignores my comment.

"She's not interesting. Like I said, it just isn't someone I pictured you with."

I stare out at the restaurant for a few seconds, filing away our conversation. I can't believe Dylan assumed Rachel was my girlfriend. She's my coach's daughter, which makes her entirely off limits, and she's still in high school—another major disqualifier. She's also not remotely my type. And Dylan's right, I would never be interested in a girl with a license plate that says HORSES. She's just asking for someone to key her car.

Do I tell Dylan the truth? My better half says yes, Gray, be honest, but my lousier half (more like three-fourths), says go with it. Embrace the bullshit. I picture Nick with a stethoscope around his head, reviving a dog and Dylan watching at his side.

Telling the truth would be the adult thing to do. But, I'm still a young adult. I'm allowed to play a few more immaturity cards.

I realize Dylan did me a huge favor by mistaking Rachel for my girlfriend. She built a wall between us, a huge medieval stone fortress ten stories high. I take a breath of relief and know I can make it through the next few days. Besides, I never technically lied about Rachel. Dylan planted the lie for me.

I push the stick shift into reverse, but out of the corner of my eye I see Dylan beginning to do the unthinkable. I grab her hand before it touches my stereo.

"Whoa. What do you think you're doing?"

Our eyes lock. Her hand is warm. Her fingertips are hot. It's like hooked bait catching me, latching on to something inside of me. I drop her fingers and her hand lingers in the air between us.

"I'm turning on the radio."

"I don't listen to radio stations. I enjoy *good* music."

"Gray, you need to listen to local radio stations on a road trip," she presses me. "It's part of the cultural experience when you're traveling."

She starts playing with the tuner until she finds a classic rock station we both agree on.

I pull out of the parking lot and Dylan is already making herself at home, digging through some maps in the side pocket of my car. She pulls out a US atlas my dad must have given me back in high school. She opens it on her lap.

"Okay," she says. "I'll be the road trip itinerary director," she announces.

"Sounds like a perfect career title for you," I say.

"It overlaps well with photography," she agrees. "Hey, do you think we could check out a rodeo? I've never seen one and I think it would be a perfect entertainment addition to our itinerary."

"This isn't a road trip, Dylan. That term suggests the idea of fun and mutual enjoyment. I would call this," I say and point to the area between us, "an extremely unfortunate predicament."

Dylan bites her lips together and stares up at the ceiling of my car. "Gray, do you want me to catch a bus?" she asks. I stop the car at a red light and consider her offer.

"I don't know," I say. "I'm still trying to accept the fact that you're sitting here right now. I'm not exactly thrilled about it. We have a tiny bit of history together."

"Look, I know this is weird," she agrees.

"Weird," I repeat. I shift gears and sail up the ramp to the highway, knowing the faster I drive, the sooner this trip will be over. The accelerator is suddenly my best friend.

"I want to try and make it fun. But if you really hate me that much, then we don't have to do this. Okay?"

I frown at her mature attitude towards my immature reaction.

"I don't hate you," I tell her and swallow. I wish that were my problem. I wish it were that easy. I look out at the endless highway spilling into the horizon. "Fine," I say, not sure what I just agreed to.

"Good," Dylan says. "So, for our first stop tonight, we can aim for—"

I raise my hand to cut her off. "Let's pull an all-nighter," I offer.

"What?" Dylan looks disappointed. "You miss out on so much when you drive at night," she argues.

"You're not going to miss out on anything, trust me," I say.

She looks out the window at flat farm fields stretched along both sides of the highway. "All the scenery vanishes. It's like you're driving in an empty, emotionless, black tunnel."

I nod. Sounds perfect.

"You call this scenery?" I ask and point around us. "Do you know what Nebraska is famous for?"

"Really big corn?" she wonders. "Corn dogs, corn chowder, corn bread, corn meal, corn—"

"It's famous for people falling asleep at the wheel. That's how not-awesome the scenery is. I can take the night shifts," I offer. "And you can sleep. Then during the day, you can drive and I'll sleep."

I smile at my Operation Avoid Dylan Plan. Activated.

She studies me. "Are you trying to avoid me?" she asks.

I answer her question by turning up the music and tuning out our conversation. I know it's a dick move, but I don't care. She has Snicker Bar to console her. And touch her. And taste her. My fingers clench around the steering wheel. Sitting so close to her, I can almost smell her skin.

I kick my car into fifth gear and we're flying down the highway and a Moody Blues song is playing on the radio. I listen to the lyrics and agree that love is only in our wildest dreams. Even when it's sitting right next to you, it always feels out of reach.

Dylan

He's doing it again. He's building a wall around his mind, a giant barricade with guards standing watch behind the parapets, weapons and arrows posed and ready to disarm at anyone daring to come through. But his mind is like a town that I've lived in and I know every street. I've memorized every turn, every slope, and every jagged hill. He can put up road blocks and build detours all he wants, but I know my way around with my eyes closed.

I look out the window as we glide by cars on the highway. I try to pass the time by focusing on the families and couples inside, or the solo drivers with eyes lost behind the mask of sunglasses. Imagining their stories helps me think outside of my own situation. I feel like we're all connected, all together on a journey through the pages of *The Illustrated History of the American Road*. But no matter how hard I try to ignore him, my eyes keep getting pulled back to Gray. His hands are wrapped tightly around the steering wheel. I know the shape of them so well. I've memorized them like a photograph pinned in the center of my mind.

Orange sunlight is sinking in the sky and it mirrors a sinking feeling inside my chest.

I remember how his lips taste. I remember his smile; how it's the most beautiful image I've ever seen. How the first time I saw him smile, on Mill Avenue in Phoenix, my head started to spin. I remember raising my camera and instinctively taking a picture, even though he was barely more than a stranger back then. All I knew was I wanted to capture that image of him. I made it my personal mission to make him smile.

"I've been listening to a lot of Counting Crows lately," I say. "You introduced me to them."

Gray doesn't look over at me, doesn't even react. He might not have heard me, but I keep going.

"I love their first album," I say and stare out at the hazy horizon. The humid air is so thick it swallows us. "They ask a lot of questions in their lyrics. They make you think. You could fill an entire journal just answering the questions in their songs."

Gray's silent. I notice his mouth tighten at the corner as if he wants to respond but he's fighting it. I'm trying to open the lock on his lips and I think talking about music can do it. It's his favorite conversation topic. He always has an opinion.

"The best song on that album is track eleven," I press. "It's all about change. How change is maybe the most important thing in life. And the hardest."

Gray's lips open and he sucks in a breath. I smile to myself. I've opened up the seam. I give myself a mental high-five.

"What did you mean when you said I White-Fanged you?" he asks.

"It's a movie reference," I say and stretch my legs and rest one of my sneakers on top of the dashboard. I look over at him. "*White Fang?*"

He starts to smile. "Isn't that the movie about a dog?"

"It's a wolf, Gray," I correct him. "A boy, played by Ethan Hawke, makes friends with a wolf. But he realizes the wolf will never be happy as a pet. It needs to be wild and free. So he pushes it away. He throws rocks at White Fang and forces him to run. He thinks he's doing the best thing for him. He just wants him to be free."

Gray pulls his eyebrows together at my description. "You mean like *Harry and the Hendersons?*" he asks and looks over at me.

This time I pull my eyebrows together. "What?"

"It's basically the same storyline, but with a Sasquatch."

"I've never heard of it."

"You've never seen *Harry and the Hendersons?*" he asks, a little condescendingly, and I shake my head. "It's one of the greatest movies of all times," he tells me. "Well, at least when you're eight." He starts to summarize the plot, how a family finds a Sasquatch on a camping trip and they bring him home and fall in love with him. But Harry never fits into their world.

"Wow," I say and shake my head at the synopsis. "What a great message."

"It's a powerful film," he agrees.

"There should be more movies with a lead Sasquatch," I say. "They exist, you know."

He nods. "I never doubted it. They're in the Pacific Northwest."

"In the Olympic National Park," I add.

"Definitely," he says.

"When I was driving through Northern California, I met a guy who saw one."

Gray's eyes flash to mine. "Shut up."

"I'm serious. He said one night he was driving on this old gravel road along the Klamath River, and rocks started hitting his car from a bluff up above. He looked up and saw a huge shadow duck under the trees." I nod with certainty. "It was Bigfoot. They're known for throwing rocks when they're feeling threatened. I guess their weaponry hasn't evolved very much."

Gray smiles at me and I immediately look away. Maybe I shouldn't have gotten him talking. Our conversations have always been my favorite foreplay. Rachel's face slams into my mind, as if her spirit is suddenly with us in the car, reminding me to behave. I see her manicured finger shaking at me. I picture her raspberry-pink stained lips. I'm impressed with women that can wear lipstick. I always lick it off.

"So, what's the family emergency?" Gray asks.

I sigh and remember this isn't truly a fun, carefree road trip.

"My sister ran away," I say.

"Serena?" he asks and I nod. "Wait, isn't she out of high school?" he asks.

"She just graduated. She's been eighteen for exactly three days. She didn't even return our birthday calls."

"She's eighteen and she's out of high school," he repeats to clarify the facts. "Then wouldn't the correct phrase be 'she moved away'?"

"It's not that easy," I tell him. "She's pregnant."

"Oh," Gray says. "That changes things."

I nod. "She got knocked up by a jerk-off," I inform him. "She never even told us. She managed to hide it from my mom all summer. They ran off together three weeks ago and all she left us was a note."

"You're trying to track her down?" he asks. "How do you know where to look?"

"He was supposed to perform in Omaha tonight, but they canceled his show. All I know is he has two shows scheduled in Flagstaff, Arizona, two days from now. So I need to get there."

"Shows? Is he a musician?"

I shake my head with disgust. "Worse. He's a stand-up comedian."

"That's cool," Gray says. "Is he funny?" I stare at Gray as if he suddenly started speaking in an unknown dialect. "Have you ever heard him perform?" he asks me.

"I don't care if he's Dane Cook," I say. "He impregnated my baby sister. She's due in two weeks and she doesn't have a permanent address. She won't answer her phone. She refuses to talk to us."

He smiles, this thoughtful, opinionated smile and now I know he has some theories.

"Does this comedian have a name or should we just call him The Impregnator?"

I start to smile but just as quickly it fades. "Mike. Mike Stone."

"What makes him such a jerk-off?" Gray asks.

"He's ten years older than Serena."

Gray looks indifferent. He waves his hand for me to continue and I frown at him.

"Isn't that bad enough?" I ask. "It's statutory rape."

"Not if it was consensual," he points out. I open my mouth to argue but he keeps going. "Maybe she threw herself at him. Maybe she lied about her age. Girls do it all the time."

"Gray—"

"Think about it. If he tours the country and he's hilarious and slightly better looking than a road sign, girls probably throw themselves at him. You know how many girls chase us after baseball games? They literally stalk our cars us like psychopaths and they think it's really cute. I want to hold up a sign that says, 'have some self-respect.'"

I can't believe he's defending Mike. Is this some kind of a bro code?

"Thanks for your thoughtful jersey chasing anecdote," I say. "It was very touching. This is different."

I sigh and stare out the front windshield. Maybe I shouldn't have opened up his tight seal. Sometimes Gray's opinions can be a little too candid. I can feel him watching me, reading into my frown. He taps his fingers on the steering wheel.

"Have your parents called the cops?" he asks.

I shake my head. "In her note, Serena said if we called the cops she'd never speak to us again. She wants to be with Mike. She thinks she's in love."

Gray nods. "Maybe the trick to ending your family feud is to start believing her," he offers.

"She's not in love," I argue. "They hardly know each other. She's just young and naïve."

He smiles and looks at me. "Isn't that what your parents used to say to you? They never took you seriously. Remember how frustrated you were?"

I reach for the music dial to turn up the volume because I'm sick of this conversation. Gray grabs my hand again.

"I've never seen you like this," he says.

"Like what?" I ask him.

"Irritated," he says and drops my hand. "You never let anything bother you. It's Serena's problem, not yours."

"I don't see it that way," I say. "It *is* my problem. We're family. This little baby is our family. Problems should never rest on one person. We'd get crushed that way. We all have to carry it now." I look out the window at the green fields that tuck themselves under the cloudy horizon. "I'm mad because Serena is being so…," my voice trails off because I hate saying the word. I hate to label my sister with such a terrible insult. I look at Gray for help.

"What do you think is the worst insult you can say to someone?" I ask him.

Gray leans his head to the side while he thinks about this. "That's a good question," he says. "Dick licker is pretty bad. Uncle fucker hits low. Although, I'm more of a purist. I think a well executed mother fucker can always cut deep."

I give him a blank stare.

"I'm thinking more along the lines of *selfish*," I say.

"Oh," he says. "Yeah, that's definitely insulting."

"That's my issue," I say. "She's not thinking about this baby. She's only thinking about herself." I look out the window and the sunset has dropped behind a wall of purple-black clouds. They glow with pockets of flashing electric lights. The spectacle matches the conflicting thoughts flashing through my head.

Gray

The horizon fills with clouds as black as soot and the sky is tinted a sickly shade of yellow. Thunder rumbles around us and the noise makes the car windows shake.

"I'm not a weather expert, but I'm sensing a very unstable air mass heading in our direction," Dylan says, looking out the window at the menacing clouds.

I play with the radio tuner, trying to find a local weather report. My hand flies off the dial when a piercing alarm fills the car speakers. It sounds like a nationwide alert that a nuclear bomb is heading our way.

A voice comes through the speaker and I brace myself for the news that the US just declared World War III, but instead a meteorologist lists all of the counties currently under a tornado warning: Polk, Fillmore, York, Hamilton, and Merrick.

My stomach knots and I hand Dylan my phone. "Can you find out what county we're in?" I ask.

She stares down at the touch screen like I just handed her a microscope and asked her to map the human genome.

"You want me to what?" she asks.

"Check our location on the map," I ask her and point to my phone. "See what county we're in."

"How?" she asks me.

"It's one of the apps," I tell her. "Haven't you learned how to use a cell phone yet?" I know she bought a flip phone last spring.

"I'm still in training," she says.

A shower of rain starts to fall in heavy sheets. A stroke of lightening flashes next to the car, answered by a crack of thunder and my fingers instinctively tighten around the steering wheel. I look out the window at green-ish black clouds racing low in the sky.

I glance impatiently at Dylan and she's scrolling through all the apps on my phone, fascinated.

"It's like a journal," she tells me. "What's the Area 51 app?"

I rub my hand over my forehead. "It's for extraterrestrial sightings," I say.

"Really?" she asks. "You believe in that stuff?"

"No," I say. "It's just entertaining."

She opens the app with the touch of her finger and starts scrolling through a featured story.

"What's a USO?" she asks.

I sigh. "It's an unidentified submersible object," I say shortly and she gives me a confused look. "You know, like an alien submarine?" I say.

"Or the Loch Ness Monster?" she asks.

Rain is starting to fall so hard it sounds like it's mixed with rocks.

"Dylan, focus!" I yell and point out the window. "Map. County. Tornado warning." Lightening crackles around us and thunder shakes the car. The rain turns to hail. It hammers the rooftop like driving nails. It's so loud I swear the windows are going to shatter.

I lean forward, trying to see out of the windshield. Dylan sets the phone down and presses her palms flat against the windshield as if she's trying to hold it up.

"It's going to crash through," she shouts and I agree with her. The hail sounds like a stream of bullets hitting our car. I look at the speedometer and I'm barely going thirty miles an hour.

"We'll be fine," I say to myself and swallow. We coast down a blurry, almost invisible road. The headlights carve a few yards of our path at a time.

A lightning bolt hits the ground with a cracking fizz and thunder screams with rage. Dylan unzips her backpack and pulls out her camera. She unbuckles her seatbelt so she can turn around to face the backseat.

"What are you doing?" I shout to be heard over the hail.

"It's one of nature's greatest photo shoots," she yells and looks over at me. "I didn't know you were scared of storms," she says.

"Not if I'm in a basement cellar. Driving through tornado valley's a little different," I shout as I struggle to keep the car steady on the flooding road.

An alarm warning wails again over the radio. As if I'm not freaked out enough, a man's voice, sounding as dark and ominous as the Gatekeeper of Hell, reports that two funnel clouds have been spotted and one tornado touched down in York county.

"SEEK SHELTER," the voice commands. I'm waiting for him to add, "OR ROT IN HELL."

Shelter. I strain my eyes to see through the curtain of rain. All I see is darkness, as if the clouds have fallen on top of us, smothering us inside.

"I should pull over," I say, and my foot eases up on the accelerator. I glance at the clock and it's only 9 PM. We've barely been driving for two hours. Operation Avoid Dylan Plan: Failure.

All of the other cars on the highway barrel along, seemingly unaffected, as if evening tornados are part of their daily work commute.

"Will you grab the wheel?" I ask Dylan. I pick up my phone and scroll for the map. The car starts to hydroplane and I grab the wheel back and my phone slips through my fingers, in between the car seat and the console.

"Crap. F—"

Mother Nature muffles my curse with a lightning bolt and simultaneous burst of thunder. She must hate profanity. The storm is on top of us, like a monster crawling at us from the sky.

"Do you have a phone?" I ask Dylan.

"It's in the trunk," she says. She rests a hand on my arm. For once, I'm not affected by her touch. Fear of death is great for defusing sexual tension.

"Gray, we're fine," she says. The hail finally quiets down, replaced by a hard rain. I search for a green exit sign in the distance.

"I grew up around these things," she says. "There are plenty of signs before a tornado hits."

"Like what?" I ask.

"First, the sky needs to turn a yellowish-green color."

I look out at the green tinted clouds. "Okay."

"There also needs to be this creepy, foreboding silence that happens right before it touches down."

I listen and it sounds like the rain is letting up. The wind gusts are subsiding. I can finally see the road clearly.

"Yeah?" I ask.

"Then, you see the funnel cloud in the sky. It starts to roll over on itself, spinning into a tight spiral just like a spider spins webbing around its victims."

I stare at her. The image is absolutely terrifying.

"Finally, the funnel cloud turns into a twister and touches the ground," she says easily, as if this science discovery conversation has nothing to do with our current scenario.

I can't take my eyes off of the road to examine the sky for funnel clouds, so I'll have to trust her on this one.

"And the last sign is, you hear the sound," Dylan says. "It's like a train. That's when you know it's time to run."

I swallow. There is an undeniable roar behind us. Dylan and I turn to look over our shoulders. In a streak of lighting we see a dangling twister in the distance.

We both scream and Dylan lifts her camera and turns to record it and I see a green exit sign ahead. I step on the accelerator.

"You should never try to outdrive a tornado," Dylan shouts.

"What's our other option? Death?" I say. The rain starts to fall harder now, mixed with hail.

"Pull over into the ditch and let me get some really great photos," she says.

"Forget it," I say. There's a light in the distance, a yellow light, and I pray that it's a gas station. A gust of wind pushes against the side of my car and for an instant it feels like the tires have left the ground.

"The good news is they only last about a minute," Dylan shouts over the rain and whistling wind.

"Thanks," I shout back to her as I try to outdrive the tornado on our tail. "I'm so happy to hear that."

In the distance a single yellow light shines through the storm like a fallen star. It's my only source of navigation.

The car wheels start to hydroplane again and I slow down long enough for the tires to catch the concrete. Dylan is still facing backwards, taking a photo documentation of the most terrifying moment of my life.

This is awful.

"This is amazing," Dylan yells.

"Is it gaining on us?" I ask.

She shakes her head. "No, it looks pretty indecisive. It keeps going back and forth. It looks like it's doing the twist. Haha, twister, doing the twist? Get it?"

I exit the highway and my car kicks up a spray of water at the stop sign. The country road is starting to flood, but I head for the yellow light. As we get closer, a farmhouse comes into view. Lights are on inside and it's all the welcome I need.

I turn onto the gravel driveway and the wheels kick up waves of water. I turn off the car and have to push my door with both hands to open it. Dylan shoves her camera in her backpack and opens her door. I stand for just a minute and feel the odd vacuum of the wind. It's as if the air is coming out of the ground, not from the sky.

I look for Dylan and she's standing on the other side of the car. She's using one hand to keep the hair out of her eyes and her other hand is pointing up at the sky. I follow her hand and in the flashes of lightening I can see two tornadoes, far off in the horizon, dancing along the ground. They spin and twist next to each other like mad lovers. I can hear the roar of the wind, like the far-off whistle of a train. It's strange to stand here, in the rain, and know that just beyond me the world is spinning wildly out of control. Being with Dylan is like that, always balancing on the edge of insanity, like riding up the slow climb of a roller coaster and waiting for the soaring ride that follows on the other side.

The wind starts to pick up and whip the air around us. I grab Dylan's hand before we're yanked off the ground. We run for the porch light, our feet splashing in puddles the size of ponds in the driveway. We jump up the stairs and open the door to a screened-in porch. The door flies back so quickly in the gust of wind it nearly rips off its hinges. When we get to the front door, we don't even have to knock.

A woman appears and smiles as if she was expecting us. She waves us inside and shuts the storm door behind us.

Dylan and I are both panting. Her hand is warm and wet inside mine. I hold it tightly, and have to remind myself to let go.

Dylan

My hand reluctantly slides out of Gray's and I almost grab it back until I remember I've lost that privilege.

"You got here just in time," the woman says. "Two tornados touched down north of here."

"We noticed," Gray says.

The woman introduces herself as Sue Anne. Her gray-ish blond hair is pinned on top of her head like a bird's nest. She introduces her husband, Chris, who looks over for a second and offers us a nod, but his eyes snap back to a baseball game on the TV. They look close to my grandparent's age.

Sue Anne asks us to take off our shoes since they're leaving wet trails on the hardwood floors. She sets them outside the front door, in the screened-in porch. Thunder rumbles and the house moans against the gusting wind but she and Chris are as oblivious to the weather as if it were a light breeze.

Sue Anne looks between me and Gray.

"How long have you two been on the road together?" she asks.

"About two hours," I say.

She laughs. "Interesting way to start off your trip."

I lift one shoulder. "Turbulence appears to be my lifestyle," I tell her and she smiles.

"Let me get you two some towels," she offers. I thank her and look out the front window at streaks of lightening that strobe through the sky. "I think being pulled into a tornado would be a romantic way to die," I say. "To get picked up in the air, and twisted inside a swirling cloud of energy. It might be really calm, really beautiful in the center. Or, maybe it's a space dimension portal," I imagine.

I look at Gray and he's watching me. "Okay, Thor," he says.

The baseball game is interrupted with an emergency weather report and Chris groans at the distraction. A radar map pops up on the screen and the entire state is covered in red, as if it's smeared in blood.

"I'm surprised you're the only ones here," Sue Anne says, returning to the entryway and handing towels to each of us. We thank her, and I twist my pigtails in the towel to wring them dry. She pulls back a white curtain, bordered in lace, to look out the window. "During this kind of weather, we always get house guests. I told my husband we should open up a hotel." She looks between me and Gray and offers us some homemade corn bread. Gray tells her no, thank you, and joins Chris to watch the forecast. But I take her up on the offer.

I follow Sue Anne down a creaking hardwood floor, bumpy and rippled from years of wear. When we walk in the kitchen I get the sensation that I'm walking downhill. The farmhouse must be ancient.

"How long have you lived out here?" I ask.

"The house has been in the family for four generations," she tells me. "We retired the farm about ten years ago, but I can't imagine living anywhere else."

"Do you have any kids?" I ask.

"Just one," Sue Anne tells me. "A daughter. And two grand kids."

She offers me a seat at the kitchen table, covered in a vinyl red and white checkered cover. It matches the checkered valiances over the kitchen windows. I sit down and examine a salt and pepper shaker in the design of farm silos. I'm still trying to wrap my mind around the fact that I'm here, stranded in the middle of Nebraska with Gray. I can still see his face in the parking lot when he recognized me. He didn't look surprised or shocked to see me. It was worse than that. He looked scared, as if he was staring at a tidal wave looming over him and he wasn't sure whether to hold his ground and pray, or run for his life.

I do what I do best when I'm emotionally overwhelmed. I spill my heart out.

I explain to Sue Anne how I've been on the road for two weeks looking for Serena, and how my car broke down in Omaha. When I mention running into Gray a few hours ago, she stops slicing bread and turns to look at me.

"You mean, you two aren't together?" Sue Anne asks.

"Oh. No," I say. Thunder rumbles outside.

"You were holding hands when you came in," she catches me.

"That's just because of the storm," I say.

"Was it?" she asks and then she cuts herself off. "Sorry. It's none of my business. My husband always says I'm a little bit psychic, but I just love observing people. They say so much without saying anything."

I smile. I feel like she's an old friend. "We used to date," I tell her. "It's a long story."

"Looks like there's still some feelings," she says, and sets down a plate in front of me.

"Yes," I say without hesitating. "I'm in love with him. Completely. Absolutely. Tragically."

She laughs. "Tragic?" she asks. "Isn't it a good thing to be in love?"

"No." I look up at her and shake my head. "It's actually the worst feeling in the world. It's agonizical."

"Is that a real word?" she asks.

"I just made it up," I say. "I tend to do that. I make up words. Sometimes there are never the right ones, you know?"

"What does agonizical mean?" she asks.

I hold up my hands like it's obvious. "To be consumed with shock and denial at unrequited love from the man who is supposed to be your soul mate," I say. I prop my elbow on the table and rest my chin in my hand. I blow out a sigh.

"Unrequited?" she says and sits down across from me. I pick up a piece of thick, yellow bread lathered in butter and I take an enormous bite. Even the whipped butter tastes sweet and homemade.

"Are you saying that man out there isn't in love with you?" she asks and points at the door. I look in the direction she's pointing, down the hallway.

"He has a girlfriend," I say through a mouthful of bread.

She laughs again. "Well, honey, I can guarantee you he's only thinking about one girl right now. And it's not his girlfriend."

I raise my eyebrows and look around her kitchen for a sign advertising psychic readings.

"How do you know?" I ask.

"There's a trick to understanding all men," she claims.

I lean closer to her over the table, intrigued.

"If you want to know what a man is thinking about just watch his eyes," she says. "Where a man's eyes go, that is where his heart is. It's like the two are linked. That's how I met my husband. We were at a party and he was with another girl at the time. But his eyes never left me. They followed me around the room all night. We were dating a week later." She points back towards the living room. "That boy's eyes have been following you since you two walked in the door."

"Probably because he thinks I'm nuts," I say, which is a much more likely hypothesis.

"They usually do, dear. It's another sign they're in love. When a man tells you that you're insane, it's really his way of professing his love."

I smile. I've never met this woman before, but I've decided she's an angel, or maybe a messenger of Fate. I stare into her brown eyes, and notice the whites are webbed with thin red spidery veins. They're beautiful and complicated and I can tell she's lived her life without ever missing a single detail.

I gulp down the corn bread with a glass of milk and my stomach is relishing the flavor and my mind is reveling in her words. Rain starts to hit the side of the window, but the storm isn't angry anymore. It's like a cleansing shower, washing away my heavy thoughts, flushing them from my mind like branches down a stream.

We head back into the living room and Gray's eyes snap to me when I walk through the door. I feel a rush of nerves ball in my stomach when our eyes meet. My body is still adjusting to the shock of his presence. A tornado warning scrolls along the bottom of the screen and we all turn to read the weather report.

"A cold front's moving through," Chris informs us. "And it's taking its sweet time. It's supposed to storm all night." The warning statement runs across the screen like a teleprompter: expect golf ball sized hail, dangerous lightening, and wind gusts up to seventy-miles-an-hour. Seek shelter. Do not go outside.

"How far is it to the nearest town?" I ask.

"About forty miles," Chris says. He takes a sip of beer. "The towns are all under flash floods. I'd consider trading in your car for a boat."

I look at Gray and notice his eyes widen.

"He's just joking around. You kids aren't going anywhere," Sue Anne says. "You're welcome to stay here tonight. Follow me," she says and Gray stands up. I walk behind Sue Anne and Gray walks a few feet behind me. When we stop in front of a closed door, he almost stumbles into me and I feel a jolt run up my back.

I've become acutely aware of space over the last few hours, how my mind and body react to the proximity of Gray. I start to mentally record my observations:

GRAY PROXIMITY SCALE:

1. **Standing in the Same Room** = Generalized anxiety, stomach flips, hyper awareness, physical need to repress the smile reflex.
2. **Three Feet Away** = Light-headedness, urge to touch magnified, noticeable face flush.
3. **One Foot Away** = WARNING—ENTERING PRZ (pheromone release zone). Body detects sex pheromones triggering sexual desire, heart spasms, tingling of nerve endings in lips, tongue and fingertips, noticeable heart palpitations, pelvic muscles contracting.
4. **Six Inches Away** = WARNING—ENTERING KZ (kissing zone). Sensory overload, heightened sense of smell, taste, and touch, elevated body temperature, hormone levels increase approximately 1,000%, shallow breath, diminished decision-making ability.
5. **Less Than Six Inches Away** = ABORT. ABORT. THERE IS NO GOING BACK.

I silently wonder if a body suit made out of steel could repel any of these symptoms.

When Sue Anne opens the guest bedroom and we walk in, Gray's mouth drops open.

I look around and feel like we stepped inside a five-year-old girl's play fort. Everything is pink. The quilt on the bed, the frilly curtains, the lamp shades, even the chair in the corner looks like it's wearing a pink tutu.

Gray's eyes are fixed on the full-sized bed, sitting in the middle of the room. I can almost see a red DO NOT ENTER warning sign emblazed over the patchwork quilt.

"I hope this will do," Sue Anne remarks.

The room's tiny. There's hardly any floor space so sleeping next to the bed isn't an option. Even the bed looks small, or maybe objects appear smaller than normal when viewed through sexual tension.

Gray points over his shoulder.

"Ah, I noticed a couch in the living room. Would it be alright if I crashed in there later?" he asks.

She shakes her head.

"Sorry, but my husband is a terrible snorer. It sounds like a snow plow's driving through our room, so I kick him out of bed around midnight. He uses the couch."

Gray nods. "No problem," he says. He meets my eyes and I shrug.

Sue Anne offers me a quick smile and a wink before she shuts the door. I smile back, but it's as weak as tissue paper. I feel terrible. Gray was nice enough to give me a ride to Flagstaff. Sharing a bed, with our past, takes our predicament from uncomfortable to painful.

I look around the room and an old fashioned wooden clock on the wall points to ten o'clock. Gray looks nowhere near tired. I'm not sure which is worse for him, being enclosed in a tiny bedroom with me for the night, or dodging tornados. They seem to be equally horrifying.

He sits down on the tutu chair. I almost raise my camera to take a picture, but I doubt Gray wants me to document the most awkward moment of his life. The small pink chair only makes his body stand out, long and dark and masculine against it. I notice the solid line of his calf muscles. I lick my lips and look away.

"Isn't this great?" I ask and sit on the corner of the bed. Gray lowers his eyebrows at my terrible joke. "We're basically getting a free room at a bed and breakfast," I point out.

He nods. "It's a perfect travel budget," he agrees. "I'll try to drive into oncoming storms more often."

I laugh and I'm grateful for the joke. At least his sarcasm is intact.

I pull out my pigtails and my damp hair falls wavy around my neck. I run my fingers through it and my hair gets caught in knots and I realize I don't have a comb. I had been borrowing Nick's the entire trip. I blow out a sigh and stare down at my naked feet, complete with a flip flop tan line. Gray used to trace his fingers over all my tan lines, like a maze, starting at my feet and working his way up, although he never made it all the way to my head. There were too many interesting detours to take along the way. I shift and look over at Gray and his eyes are on me. I think about what Sue Anne said. I expect him to snap his gaze away, but he doesn't. More thunder rumbles outside.

"Are you having your deep thought for the day?" he asks me.

"Today I've had too many to count," I admit. I wish I could share my spatial proximity data analysis with him. I know he'd appreciate it.

"Since when is your hair wavy?" he asks, studying me.

"When I cut it short, it just got wavy. I guess when it's longer it straightens out." I smile. "Even my hair can't make up its mind."

Gray keeps his eyes on mine.

"Snicker bar's probably worried about you," he says.

So, that's what he's thinking about. No, Nick isn't worried about me. He would be ecstatic to hear about my current situation, and enraged that I'm not taking full advantage of it.

"Probably," I say and try to tussle the knots out of my hair with my fingers.

"Sorry if I was being a jerk earlier today," Gray says. I meet his eyes, surprised by the apology. "I was a little shocked to see you and then meet your boyfriend," he admits. "It was a lot to take in."

I open my mouth to cut him off. I can't lie to him about Nick. It's time to come clean.

"Gray—"

"But, he's good for you," Gray says with a satisfied nod as if this is a theory he's recently comes to terms with.

I look down at the floor and feel my forehead crease with confusion. What? He's condoning our relationship? That doesn't make sense. Sue Anne is no longer a messenger of Fate. She is a messenger of Bullshit.

I look back at him. "Why do you think that?" I ask.

"I don't know," Gray says.

His unresponsive response annoys me.

"Yes, you do," I say. "You brought it up. You have a hundred opinions about everything."

"True," he says. He breathes out a long, thoughtful breath and his chest rises and falls. He's too relaxed. Too okay with my fictional boyfriend.

"He seems more like you. Upbeat, optimistic, light-hearted. Loves dogs and appreciates shitty cars." He smiles. It makes me frown. I realize what he's saying.

I lean forward and rest my elbows on my knees. "You think that's what makes a relationship work? For two people to be alike?"

"Maybe," he says. "That's one thing that always bothered me when we were dating. I always felt like I wasn't positive enough for you," he admits.

I think about the absurdity of his words. I love his deep thoughts. I love his theories; they're fascinating because they're the opposite of mine. It's like I'm upside-down when I'm around him, seeing things from an entirely different perspective. Gray challenges me—it's what I love most about him.

"Do you think it ever bothered me?" I ask him.

"No, but it bothered me," he says. "I don't want to feel like I'm stealing from you. I don't want to drain all your happy juice."

This is his most ridiculous theory to date.

"Did it ever occur to you that I was happy because of *you*?" I ask him. "That you helped bring out that side out of me? That you were the main ingredient of my 'happy juice?'"

"No," he says simply. He sits back in the chair and stretches out his legs. His feet are a few inches away from mine. "I'm never going to be like you, Dylan."

"How are we so different?"

He laughs. "How are we not different? You love everyone, and I immensely dislike most people. You love everything and pretty much everything annoys me to some level. I have to work to see things positively. You just have to open your eyes."

"I do hate things," I say. "I hate Super Bowl parties. Parades. Dresses. Zoos. The circus."

"When have you seen a circus?" he asks, doubting my sincerity.

"I haven't and I don't intend to. It's basically a traveling zoo. And I have an unexplained fear of clowns."

Gray smiles and it charges me with energy. It's suddenly hard to stay seated. His smile is like fuel.

"Besides, you love all the right things," I continue. "You love your friends. You love your family, you love good music and good food and you love me more than anyone I've ever met." He winces when I say this, and I catch myself. "I mean, you used to. You have the biggest heart of anyone I know. You just don't see it. But I think you're a better person than I am," I admit.

"That's insane," he tells me. My heartbeat picks up when I hear the word come out of his mouth. I remind myself, he didn't say *I* was insane. But it's still promising.

"You always put people first," I say. "And I don't. I put myself first. I have for years. That's one of the reasons why I dropped everything to go after Serena. If I hadn't met you, I probably wouldn't have done it. But if something like that had ever happened to your sister, you would have left everything to go after Amanda."

Gray nods because he knows I'm right. Maybe being alike isn't what's best. It's bringing out the best in each other that matters.

I open my backpack and throw a few things on the bed, looking for my overnight clothes and the toiletries shoved in the bottom. Gray surprises me and sits down on the bed next to me. It squeaks under the additional weight. My internal radar informs me Gray has entered PRZ. I sit on my hands and cross my legs. I try to ignore all my heightened nerve endings.

He reaches for a square CD case next to me. He recognizes it. He opens it and flips through the discs and my cheeks feel hotter than a sunburn. There are ten CD's inside, all mixes he made for me three summers ago.

He looks at me and I suddenly feel naked under his eyes.

"It's great road trip music," I say, trying to keep it light.

"These are three years old," he says. "Aren't you getting sick of them?"

Never.

"Maybe a little. You should make me some new ones," I say and he just looks away. I zip my backpack shut before he notices anything else inside. He leans back on his hands and his eyes trail around the room for a couple of seconds. I watch his chest rise and fall when he breathes. He looks so calm and relaxed while I feel like my blood's on fire.

"Tell me your bedroom never looked like this," he says.

I shake my head. "I never really liked pink. I think it even makes flowers look fake."

"What does your bedroom look like?" he asks me.

I meet his eyes. "My bedroom?" I ask.

"Back at home," he says. "In Wisconsin," he clarifies in case I forgot where I'm from.

"Why do you want to know?" I ask.

He shrugs and looks around the room. "It's just something I never asked you about," he says. "And I always wondered. Probably because you never settle down, so I was always trying to imagine what a 'settled down Dylan' looks like."

I think back to my parent's ranch-style house in central Wisconsin.

"It's a sewing room now," I say.

"Tell me one random thing you had in it," Gray says.

"A sex swing," I say and he raises his eyebrows.

I laugh and he smiles back. I think about the things my mom agreed to stow away in the attic. "You'd probably appreciate my Jack Black box," I say.

"Your what?"

"It's a big, black filing box I kept in my room." I explain that I named it after Jack Black because, A) he's a brilliant actor and musician, 2) he's hilarious, and D) he doesn't care what anybody thinks of him. His self-esteem has a black belt in jujitsu.

"Okay," Gray says with a nod. "I've listened to enough Tenacious D to agree with his musical talent."

"And his acting?" I ask.

"I've seen *High Fidelity*," Gray says. "And *Tenacious D and the Pick of Destiny*. Point made."

"Well, I was thinking of *Nacho Libre* and *School of Rock*, but whatever," I say. "So, starting in middle school, if I was upset or insecure about something, or having a bad day, I wrote down my problem on a piece of paper, folded it up and put it in my Jack Black box. Then I latched the box closed and stopped thinking about it. Problem solved. Jack took care of it for me."

"Do you still have it?" Gray asks.

I nod. "I wouldn't let my mom throw it away. That one was a keeper."

The rain picks up outside. It hits and slams against the window, but I think it sounds like music—a light mix of tambourine and cymbals. The wind sounds like a guitar, all low, melancholy notes. Thunder takes the drums. I'm quiet as I listen to the song.

"Posters?" he asks.

"None."

"Really? I took you for a poster kind of girl."

I shake my head. "No, I was more into clothes pins."

"What?" he asks and waits for more.

"Clothes pins," I say, like it's a normal decorating feature. "I had strings strung along all four walls of my room and I used clothes pins to hang stuff. Magazine cut outs, drawings, photographs. One fall I had an entire room full of leaves. That one got messy. I had to promise my mom never to hang organic material again."

I look over at Gray and he's suddenly too close. He's dangerously entering my KZ— his face and lips are close enough to reach out and touch. He must be trying to torture me. I try to focus on the conversation. "One wall was dedicated to missing pieces. Just random things I found—torn paper, ripped notes, receipts, bags."

"You mean garbage? You hung garbage on your walls?"

"They weren't garbage," I argue. "They were the lost remnants of a larger story." I throw up my hands. "I'm not saying interior decorating was ever my calling, Gray."

He smiles and I smile. I could step inside his smile and live there because it's one of the most familiar places I know. I could easily lean forward into him. I'm starting to, I feel our faces inching closer when suddenly the door knocks open. Gray and I turn to see Sue Anne walk inside. When she sees us sitting on the bed, her face brightens.

"Are you two cozy in here?"

"Very cozy, thanks, Sue Anne," I say.

"This is my daughter's old room," she says and looks around with nostalgia. "She loved pink. I haven't had the heart to redecorate."

"It's perfect," I say.

"Well, alright. Sweet dreams. And if you hear any sirens, you can head down to the basement if you want. It's the last door at the end of the hall." She closes the door and I hear it click shut.

Gray stands up and suddenly it's easier to breath. He stretches his arms over his head. "I'm going to grab my bag from the car," he says. "You need anything?" I shake my head. I have a toothbrush in my backpack, and a t-shirt and shorts.

When Gray leaves, I open my backpack and take out *The Giving Tree*, a book that he gave me when we first met. It's the book I didn't want him to see. I've been writing in it since he gave it to me, using it as a type of journal. It's where I keep my un-want list.

I try to un-want things. It's my latest challenge. And I'm continually broke, so it works out. Every day people make lists of the things they want, or the things they need. Shopping lists, to-do lists, grocery lists. I make it a challenge to un-want things. To see what I can do without. I un-want new shoes and make do with my dirty, worn out ones. I glue the soles together and sew holes. I un-want a new backpack and sew a patch on the one I have. Casting something away it easy, but just because it frays, just because it shows signs of age doesn't mean it's worthless. It's amazing how well things hold up if you give them extra love.

I un-wanted getting a haircut and let it grow wild until I cut it myself. I un-want makeup and let my freckles stand out. And strangely, in all the unneeding, I seem to gain more.

I look up at the door Gray just walked out of. No matter how hard I try, I can't un-want you. I can't un-need you. Sometimes we don't know what we need until we're shown what we need. Up until then, we're only making blind guesses. Sometimes, even when we think we're roaming, we're just traveling in a long circle that eventually leads us home.

Gray

I walk into the bedroom and sit down on the bed. Dylan isn't here; it gives me a chance for a mental pep talk. I run my hands through my hair. I have to mentally rise above this situation. I can't let myself remember. I can't let myself want her. She is the one thing I can never have.

I look up at the door she's about to walk through. I gave you up. I wasn't born to love you. I was born to lose you. You are my sad song. My melancholy mix. You were my past until you suddenly crashed into my present. But you will never be my future.

I replay that sentence over and over in my head.

I stare at the edge of the bed where she was sitting, sprawling her legs out like weapons. Her long, slender feet brushed against the hardwood floor like a dessert that I wasn't allowed to touch, only to see.

You can feel the energy of sexual tension. It's like a belt tied around your chest, slowly tightening. It's as if molecules in the air are lightly stinging your skin. You become aware of every inch of your body, from the back of your neck, to your toes. You are fully awake, fully exposed and bordering on the edge of pain.

A few minutes later Dylan walks into the room and shuts the door. She's wearing a dark green t-shirt and a pair of orange shorts that say Tennessee up the side of one leg. It's the furthest thing from sexy a girl could wear. The t-shirt is so baggy it looks like it hardly touches her skin, just around her throat and chest, and my eyes linger at those spots until I pull them away.

She hops onto the bed and it creaks beneath her. I look over at her and she doesn't seem the least bit weirded out, like life is just one long slumber party to her. Does this girl even feel sexual tension?

I pull the sheets back and we both climb under. I lie down on my back and keep my body as straight as a ruler. Even my toes are pointing forward.

Over the past year, I figured out a way to stop thinking about Dylan. The trick was not to think at all. As long as I filled my head with constant music and my life with distractions then I was fine. I only thought about her during the narrow cracks of silence, so I filled those cracks, cemented them tight and kept her out. I thought I could turn her invisible, as if she never existed. But all of our memories are my favorites. How do you forget your best times? How do you block out the best version of yourself? I can't freeze memories that hot. They always thaw out and run wild again.

Dylan turns off a pink lamp on the bedside table and my eyes start to adjust to the dark room. I can hear thunder grumbling outside. I feel safer in the darkness; it's like hiding under a protective blanket, blocking

Dylan out. Until she speaks and reminds me she's less than a foot away.

"Do you still think about Amanda?" she asks.

I stare up at the ceiling. Rain lightly taps against the window. Distant lightening flashes outside and illuminates the walls with flickering blue light.

"Yeah, all the time."

"Is it getting easier?" she asks.

No one's ever asked me this before. I think about her question and nod slowly. "It doesn't hurt as much," I say. "I don't feel sick to my stomach anymore. That was the worst part. It was like my body was filled with acid. My stomach always felt like it was twisting."

Dylan laces her fingers together on top of the blanket, over her chest.

"How do you feel now?" she asks.

"I'm not angry anymore," I say. "I used to be so mad. I was mad at my parents for letting Amanda drive that night. I was mad at all of Amanda's friends for inviting her to that party. I was mad at the doctors because they couldn't save her. I was mad at God for stealing her, at the road workers for leaving that patch of hidden ice on the highway. I was mad that it was so sunny and beautiful out the day after she died. It's crazy all the things you find to blame."

The rain grazes the window like sand. It's so soft it's no longer a storm, just the illusion of a storm. Thunder rumbles a lullaby in the distance.

"I still miss her like crazy," I say. "That feeling will never go away. But I don't want it to. She deserves to have me miss her every day for the rest of my life."

I look over at Dylan and I feel the medieval fortress crack and crumble. It's a worthless pile of debris against her stare. I forgot how well she knows me, how her questions are like keys and she knows just the right ones to use to pick my locks. My feet start to relax, beginning at my toes and loosening up to my ankles. My knees turn outwards, closer to her. My back and shoulders finally sink against the contours of the mattress.

"Thanks for asking about her. You're the only one who does," I say.

"It's not exactly an easy conversation," Dylan points out.

I shake my head. "People avoid it all the time, like they're afraid I'm going to fall apart and start sobbing. But you were right when we first met, you called it. I needed to talk about Amanda."

A quiet minute rolls by. Dylan's looking up at the ceiling and she sighs.

"I'm not tired," she says and turns her head to look at me. Neither am I. Usually when we're in bed together we're naked and any talking we do consists of an afterglow sex recap or foreplay sex talk. This is new for us.

"Tell me one random thing you did this year," she says. I smile as an idea comes to mind.

I look over at her. "I called the Humane Society last summer to check in on Boba."

Her eyebrows fly up when I mention the dog that we volunteered to take on walks the summer we met. "You did?"

I nod. "I was going to offer to walk him when I was visiting my parents, if he was still around."

"What did they say?" she asks, her voice rising, her eyes widening.

"They said, 'Boba isn't with us anymore.'"

Dylan gasps and slaps a hand over her mouth. I pry it away and she squeezes my fingers.

"No—" she says and I interrupt her before I see tears.

"He got adopted," I say and let her hand go.

"He did?" Dylan exclaims and I nod.

"An older couple adopted him. They wanted a very *mellow* dog," I say.

"Perfect," she says.

"They said Boba really perked up after we took him out. We gave him a second chance."

I can see her eyes widen in the darkness. "I can't think of a more wonderful bedtime story," Dylan says. "We need to do that again sometime," she insists and I just look up at the ceiling. I don't nod, but I don't disagree.

Dylan's quiet and her breathing turns long and repetitive and I know she faded off to sleep. And I'm still nowhere near it. I hear the wooden clock chime and remind me of quarter hours, half hours, full hours slipping by and I can't shake the feeling that I'm wasting time, lying here. I listen to Dylan breathe between the claps of thunder. Visions of the last three years play in my head, and I'm remembering all the good times, all the reasons why I loved her, why I still love this girl. I want my brain to remember the times that she left me, the times she made me wait, made me doubt, broke my heart. But my mind refuses to acknowledge those memories.

The clock's ticking starts to sound angry. It's an impatient tapping.

I roll over onto my stomach and rest on my elbows so I can look out the window behind the headboard. I watch the way the early dawn slowly reveals things outside: a roof on a shed, a white clothes line, a chicken coop, a white fence bordering a garden. I've gotten used to watching the sun rise and it's becoming my favorite time of the day. There's always a sense of starting over. Erasing mistakes. The air is at its calmest in the morning. It's like even the sky is meditating, staying still, keeping a clear head and focusing on the moment before it's forced to stretch and wake up. I like to think my mind can be the same way.

I look over at Dylan and her face is inches away from mine. I openly stare at her, at the angle of her nose, slightly turned up, at the long brown and black lashes feathering her eyes.

I lay down on the pillow and I can already feel the heat of the morning sun stretching into the sky.

Dylan

I walk out to the screened-in porch where Sue Anne set our shoes out to dry. I reach down to grab mine and my arm freezes inches from the wood-beamed floor. The laces of my shoes are tangled together, in the shape of a heart. I crouch down and look at the heart, solid yet so delicate. If I lightly poked the laces, I would distort the whole image. There's only one way to make it permanent.

I pull my camera out of my backpack and snap a picture. As my camera clicks, a piece of knowledge slips into place. I look between my shoes and the heart. It took all this traveling, all this time, to understand that my journey has never been about getting to a particular place. It was always a road leading to Gray. The star on my map, in my heart. My greatest tether, always letting me go but pulling me back. I've traveled 2,000 miles this summer, but that's nothing compared to the mileage I've made in my head. Thoughts are your heart's footprints, and mine always lead back to him.

I put my camera away and stare down at the heart. Wisdom is a strange teacher. She likes to show up after you make a mistake so she can point out where you went wrong, but it's too late to go back and correct it. Maybe she wants you to screw up so you're smart enough to start listening. Or, maybe Wisdom is a like a map. She always has a plan if you follow her directions.

I slip on my shoes and tie the laces and walk outside. Rays of sunshine spill through thick, gray clouds breaking up across the sky. Everything is shining with the polish of rain. The wet ground gleams in the light. The air smells like earth and wet gravel and wood. I inhale a deep breath and feel a wish taking root in my heart. I wish everything could start new with Gray.

I walk around the farmyard and I like the emptiness of this place. The puddles on the gravel are as still as mirrors. In the daylight it's clear the old farmhouse is past its prime. Its light yellow paint is blistered and chipped, and the red barn is missing patches of shingles on the roof. It's obviously been out of commission for a long time, but I can see why they never left. It must be nice to wake up every day under so much uninterrupted expanse of sky. There is something wonderfully calming about being at the center of nothing. I could live out here. I would spend every day in tank tops and jeans and sunshine. I'd take baths in a water barrel. I'd learn how to bake and garden and can vegetables. I'd sleep on the porch at night.

"I'm surprised you're not taking a million pictures right now," Gray says. I turn around and he's standing a few feet away from me. He's wearing black mesh shorts and a blue UNM baseball t-shirt that matches his eyes.

"It's perfect," I agree. "But I don't think a camera could capture it. It's more of the feeling you get when you're standing here. It's all the smells. And the silence."

"What does a rainbow smell like, exactly?" he asks and I turn and follow his gaze. There's a rainbow arched over the eastern sky. Each color stands out individually and it makes me think of piano notes, starting low and getting higher to match each of the colors. The colors even look like they have texture. Some are more fuzzy, some smoother, some matted, some shiny. The arch combines the blue sky with the dark clouds in one colorful frame.

I instantly pull my camera out of my backpack. I look through the lens, but I can't do the picture justice on the ground. I need a higher angle. I climb up on the roof of Gray's car and he doesn't stop me—I've done it before—and I find a frame clear of the electrical lines and trees that were blocking the shot. I sit down on top of his car roof for a few seconds. I look at each solid color and it makes me think about people. If we color-coordinated our feelings, our personality, what would we look like? I would be a lot of yellows, oranges and reds. Gray would be darker on the spectrum, grays and blues and greens. And that is why we are perfect. We complement each other. We complete the spectrum.

But rainbows never last. They only appear for a few spellbinding minutes, long enough to entrance you with the kind of beauty life is capable of creating, but they are never permanent. They are just a rare phenomenon when all the right elements line up, when light is separated into its most beautiful form—when the timing is absolutely perfect.

I'm afraid to blink. I don't want it to disappear.

Gray climbs up onto the hood of his car. He bends down and grabs my camera and looks through the lens before he hands it back to me.

"That's a good shot," his says and sits down next to me. Our feet dangle over the side of the roof.

"Too bad they don't last forever," I say.

"You wouldn't appreciate them if they did," Gray says.

I wonder if he's right.

"It looks like nature's Mohawk," I say.

Gray smiles. "Maybe nature recently joined a punk band," he says.

We're interrupted when Sue Anne walks out carrying a loaf of corn bread. I wonder if it's used as bartering currency in this state. We jump down off the roof and she offers me the bread and a hug. She hands me a piece of paper with her email address scribbled on it.

"Stay in touch, Dylan," she says and I promise I will. She leans in close and whispers, "Let me know how it turns out. About my theory, I mean."

Gray

We stop for breakfast in Hebron, Nebraska. Coming into town, we pass a billboard that informs us Hebron is famous for having the "World's Largest Porch Swing." I wonder if it lures a lot of tourists. Of course, Dylan insists we drive the extra two miles to the city park to see it. We pull over and walk through the thick green grass. The park is empty and the giant bench looms in the center. It looks like four wooden benches have been glued together and attached to a red metal frame. It's longer than a Greyhound bus.

We stand in front of the metal monstrosity.

"Who thinks up these things?" Dylan wonders.

"Probably someone related to you," I tell her. I lie down on the seat and barely take up a quarter of the bench and Dylan snaps my picture. She tries to rock me, but the giant swing barely moves. She groans and pushes as hard as she can and the bench wobbles in response. I kick my feet against the pavement below and try to get it going, but the metal chains only moan and squeak.

Dylan hands me her camera and sits down at the very end of the bench. I snap a picture of her from a side angle. She's so far away, she almost disappears in the back of the shot.

"All it's missing is the world's largest front porch," she says as she hops up. I hand her the camera and we head back to the car. It's so unnatural to walk next to Dylan without touching her. I suddenly don't know what to do with my hands. I concentrate on the shadows of leaves painted on the ground by the bright sunlight.

We drive back to the interstate and stop at a roadway restaurant called Mamma's Place. It shares a parking lot with a taxidermist, which makes sense since I'm sure most people are in the mood to eat after handling dead animals. A banner stretches between the two businesses that says, "You Kill It, We Fill It."

How appetizing.

In the window of the taxidermist, I notice there's a sale going on for mounted deer heads. I also notice the venison sausage is on special at Mamma's Place, according to a white board on the sidewalk. I point out this unsettling fact to Dylan.

"You might want to avoid ordering meat in this place," she says. When we walk in, I look around at all of the stuffed squirrel bodies and deer heads that clutter the restaurant walls and shelves. I assume they get a discount.

The restaurant is filled with local patrons in cowboy hats and dirty baseball caps. Denim appears to be the rural fashion trend. I realize why it's so busy—we've made the early bird special.

Dylan scoots into a booth and I almost slip in right next to her out of habit, until I remember she isn't mine and I have a pretend girlfriend and Dylan has an over-achieving, smart, outdoorsy boyfriend who could model for a Patagonia catalogue with all his stupid dogs. I hope they get married and own a dog shelter together and start a reality show about their stupid, charitable, perfect life.

For some reason, I feel the pathetic need to annoy Dylan, because her presence is sexually annoying the crap out of me. I had a hard-on three times last night, and one this morning. It's like a headache in my pants.

Dylan opens her menu and I open mine and the waitress comes up and asks if we're ready to order. I order coffee and Dylan orders lemonade, and then I clear my throat.

"I have a question," I ask the waitress, but I pin my eyes directly on Dylan's. "I was wondering which was *moister.*" I say moister slowly and delicately, giving every consonant and vowel carful enunciation. "The cinnamon rolls, or the muffins?"

Dylan scrunches her nose like she smells something foul. When we first met she told me what her three least favorite words were. Her long term memory sucks, but mine is prolific. It's one of my weaknesses. I remember everything. The challenge is to try and forget.

I look away from Dylan and smile at the waitress, an elderly woman who appears to have more red lipstick on her teeth than on her lips. She chews on the end of her pen while she considers my question.

"By moister, you mean?"

"I mean exactly that," I say. "Moist, as in having a spongy, porous texture saturated in pockets of moisture."

Dylan covers her mouth with one hand like she's about to gag. She takes a long breath and blows it out slowly between her fingers.

"Ah-huh," the waitress mumbles. "The homemade raspberry muffins are popular," she offers.

"Great," I say. "I'll have one."

I smile at Dylan's frown. This is going to be fun. Hey, if I have to be mentally, emotionally, and sexually tormented by her presence, than the least I can do is return the torture. I'm mature like that.

Dylan narrows her eyes after the waitress walks away. "Is it torture-Dylan day?" she asks. "I hate the m-word. Passionately hate."

"I know," I tell her. "You hate the words moist, protoplasm and membrane."

She sets her menu down on the table. "How do you know that?" she asks, her eyes suspicious, as if I was reading her diary.

"You told me," I remind her. "When we first met."

She blinks with surprise, trying to recall the memory. "I don't remember saying that."

I shrug. "I do."

"What else do you remember?" she asks.

I stare at her. "Everything. It's my curse."

"Wow," she says. "I have trouble remembering anything. Names. Places. Dates. I barely passed freshman history."

Must be nice. "That's probably why you take so many pictures," I tell her. "It's your way of remembering."

She smiles at me, a Dylan smile that's part lips and part laugh and it always catches the corners of my lips and pulls them up. Even when I fight to hold them down.

The waitress comes back with coffee for me and lemonade for Dylan. She slides a muffin down on the table.

"Did you decide on breakfast?" the waitress asks. Dylan orders the apple pancakes and I stall.

"Well, again, I'm just looking over your menu," I say, "and I'm wondering which is moister, the pancakes or the waffles?

"Um, the French toast is popular. I think it's moist," the waitress offers.

"Sounds great," I say. I close my menu and hand it to her. "I'll have that."

She nods and sticks her pen behind her ear and walks away.

I look down at the giant muffin. Its billowing top is as big as the entire plate. I peel a piece off and stick it in my mouth. "Mmm, that is the moistest muffin I have ever had."

I start to laugh and Dylan narrows her eyes. "I bet I can make you a hundred times more uncomfortable than you could ever make me," she says.

I shake my head. "I know you too well," I say. "Nothing you do can surprise me."

She raises her eyebrows. "Is that a dare?" she asks.

"Sure," I say.

She wipes her fingers slowly across her napkin. She dabs the corners of her mouth clean and I start to regret my words.

She scoots out of the booth and stands up. She straightens her t-shirt over her jean shorts. She walks into the center of the narrow isle, between our booth and the line of tables, turns to me, and clears her throat.

Oh, no.

"HAPPY BIRHTDAY TO YOU," she belts out in low vibrato, like a baritone opera singer. She's not trying to sound good, she's going for loud. Embarrassingly, nauseatingly loud. Her voice echoes off of the walls. She sounds exactly like Chevy Chase singing *Joy to the World* in the movie *Christmas Vacation*. I can feel every pint of blood in my body rush to my face.

"HAPPY BIRTHDAY TO YOU," she continues. Every conversation in the restaurant has ceased and every pair of eyes is on me. I swear even the deer heads look alarmed. I cross my arms over my chest and stare at Dylan. Her eyes are beaming down at me.

"HAPPY BIRTHDAY, DEAR, SHELDON."

I glare up at her. Of course she has to give me a lame ass name. The cooks are out of the kitchen, staring and smiling. I feel myself sinking into the booth seat. I contemplate hiding underneath the table.

"HAPPY BIRTHDAY TO YOU." Dylan rings out the final line with an exaggerated vibrato and a sweeping arm motion that ends with a deep bow. The restaurant rips into applause and laughter. Dylan turns and waves to the patrons before she sits down. She calmly picks up her fork and helps herself to my muffin.

She's quiet and I wonder if she ripped a vocal chord with her little dramatic performance. I almost wish she did.

"We had an Olympic-style truth or dare competition in my neighborhood every summer when I was growing up," Dylan tells me. She points both of her thumbs at her chest. "Eight year, gold medal winner," she says. "Dare with care."

I set both of my hands on the table. "I promise I will never say the m-word for as long as I live," I tell her. "Just, please, swear on your mother's life that you will never sing like that again."

"Was it that terrible?" she asks.

"The worst thing I've ever heard," I say.

She smiles like I paid her a compliment.

"Okay, truce," she says. "Pinkie swear." She holds out her hand but I shake my head.

"Thumb swear," I say.

"What?"

"It's much more sincere than a pinkie swear," I tell her.

She sticks her thumb out and I wrap my thumb around hers and squeeze. My hand starts to tingle from the connection and I drop her thumb with annoyance and glare at my hand. Apparently even her thumb turns me on. God, can you cut me a break, here?

"Amanda coined that swear," I say. "She owns the patent, so you can't use it unless you're family." I drink my coffee and Dylan sucks down half of her lemonade.

"Happy Birthday, Sheldon," an older woman says to me as she passes our booth. I politely nod in response.

"You don't wear baseball caps anymore," Dylan notes.

"I shaved my hair," I say. "It doesn't get in my eyes."

She smiles. She knows me better than that.

"That's not why you wore hats," she says. "You're letting more in."

"Maybe," I admit.

"You've changed a little bit," she says.

Our waitress brings our food and informs us a customer paid for our bill. She offers me more coffee, but I shake my head.

"Have a great day, Sheldon," she tells me and pats me on the shoulder. When she walks away I roll my eyes at Dylan.

"Sheldon?" I ask her. "Really? The singing wasn't bad enough?"

"Hey, we just stretched our travel budget," Dylan points out, as if I should thank her.

"I get the feeling freebies are common for you."

She lifts her hands. "Life loves improv," she informs me. "The more dares you're willing to take on, the better."

I back pedal to her earlier comment. "So, how have I changed?" I ask her.

She sits back in the booth and studies me. "I can't quite place it. There are the obvious physical changes. Beer gut. Double chin. Receding hair line."

I laugh with amusement and it makes her smile.

"You're more relaxed," she says. "Maybe even happy?"

I don't disagree with her. But I don't tell her why I'm relaxed. Why I'm happy. Her energy has always had that effect on me. She energizes me but in a completely calming way, like lying out in the sun, feeling your insides heat up, all the way to your core.

"You must be happy you played so well this season," Dylan guesses. "I heard you say you got VIP?"

"MVP, Dylan," I correct her.

"Right. Or maybe it's because of Rachel?" she suggests.

I lock eyes with her and Guilt stomps hard on my chest and it makes my shoulders tense. He must wear steel-plated boots. But I ignore his persistent kick. Rachel is the only wall I have left. It's my only line of defense right now.

"It's something else," I admit. "I'm starting to get why you like traveling so much."

"Why's that?" she asks.

"It's just freeing. Going to a brand new place where no one knows you. You get a fresh start. It's like you purge your old life and you're new again. You get to reinvent yourself."

She nods. "Everyone needs to do it. People get so domesticated."

"That's because we're designed to domesticate," I point out. "We're not wild animals. We have this whole evolutionary gap with apes for a reason."

Dylan gives me an unbelieving stare. "But maybe we are wild," she says. "I think deep down, in the oldest part of our reptilian brains, we still have that instinct in us. I think we're meant to be wild, at least for a while."

She makes a good point.

"Don't you ever feel like you're running away, when you're leaving all the time, when you never stay in one place for very long?" I ask her.

"No. I'm not running away," she says. "I'm just on my own path. It's hard to explain because it's uncharted. It isn't paved out and marked with street routes. It's invisible to everybody *but* me. I think that's the best part about it."

I listen to her talk and her words slide into places inside of me. They fill empty spaces and cracks like caulking fills holes and I'm nodding in agreement.

"Moving to New Mexico was the best thing I ever could have done," I tell her. "And I get to leave every summer to play baseball. It's almost too easy. I feel like I'm cheating. I get to leave all my problems behind, shove them in a closet and forget about them."

"It gets old though," she says and finishes her last bite of pancakes. "And your problems always resurface, no matter how deep you bury them." I'm surprised to hear this.

"That doesn't sound like White Fang talk."

She shrugs. "The last time I was home, I spent a couple of hours just walking around my house. I was enamored with our basement. My parents have a storage room with all these boxes of decorations labeled for every holiday. They're in neat stacks piled all the way to the ceiling. It made me jealous." She sets her elbow on the table and rests her chin in her hand. Her eyes turn thoughtful. "I wonder what that would be like," she says.

My forehead creases. "To have a holiday decoration box?"

She laughs. "To have some consistency. Rituals. Traditions. My only tradition is to be nontraditional."

I smile and swipe the last smudge of syrup off my plate with a piece of toast.

"After a while it's nice to be around people that get you," she says. "Starting over all the time, making new friends, it gets exhausting. When nobody knows you it's hard to even know yourself."

I read into all the things she's not saying. Is Dylan considering settling down?

"Do you think you'll ever go back to college?" I ask.

"I went to a class this spring," she tells me. "I was living in Minneapolis, and one of my friends was a student, so I went with her to experience this whole 'college phenomenon' everybody talks about."

"And?" I ask.

"They were all introductory courses," Dylan says. "Intro to biology or intro to drawing. I watched people study in coffee shops, quizzing each other with note cards, memorizing words that mean nothing to them. Real life isn't like that. You don't get ABCD options. You can't fill in the blanks of your life. It's maddening if you think about it. Life doesn't start out easy and eventually get harder. Life asks really hard things of you, right away. That's what I love about it. Life's the best teacher."

"So what are you going to do next?" I ask.

She lifts her shoulders. "I'm still trying to figure that out."

I try again.

"What's your final destination?"

She meets my eyes. She knows what I'm asking.

"Flagstaff," she says.

I nod slowly. That's all the validation I need. She's still a drifter, a dreamer, an ambling vagabond. She doesn't plan five minutes into the future. She can't follow an outline for her life. She's only capable of letting it unfold, one scene at a time. Dylan hasn't changed. I doubt she ever will.

I leave a ten dollar tip on the table and slide out of the booth. I follow Dylan outside where the sun is already beating down on the black top. Even after a cup of coffee, my eyelids are heavy. I hand her my car keys.

"It's your shift," I tell her. When we get in the car, I text my parents to let them know I survived the tornado apocalypse. I'm surprised Dylan hasn't texted Snickerdoodle yet. But then I remember Dylan's attachment to people is out of sight out of mind. Nick might as well get used to it.

PART TWO: THE DETOUR

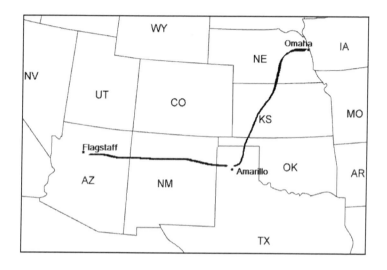

Gray

I wake up to music pouring through the speakers and the sun is glaring in my eyes like it's mad at me for sleeping the morning away. I squint out the window at the farm fields bordering the highway, scorched and brown from the summer sun.

I hear the song *Faith* playing, by George Michael. If Dylan is right, and listening to local radio stations is a cultural experience, then it appears most of America is stuck inside an 80's time warp.

I twist in the seat. My neck's stiff from attempting to sleep and hold my head up at the same time. I blink at the dashboard clock with surprise. It's already past noon. I look out the front window at a beige highway that seems to never end, just repeat itself over and over with monotony and sun-bleached billboards advertising fast food restaurants and hotel chains. It feels like we're going nowhere, just circling a wide track of road. I suddenly feel too constrained. My knees are pinned. My legs want to stretch. I stare out at the western horizon and I just want to get to Arizona. I want to put distance between me and Dylan. I want to drop her off and drive away without ever looking back and think, finally, forever, we are DONE.

"Isn't the open road great?" I hear Dylan say. "It's like having wings."

I turn my neck and wonder if Dylan is talking to me, or to herself. I watch her take a bite of red licorice, and then use it as a drum stick against the steering wheel to match the acoustic rhythm of the song. She's nodding her head, singing along to the lyrics.

I stretch my arms out and Dylan notices and says, "Hey, look who decided to join us."

I wrinkle my forehead and wonder what she means by *us*, as if she has an imaginary friend or a split personality. Either scenario wouldn't completely surprise me. Dylan has always hovered dangerously between being mildly insane and having a full blown personality disorder.

I'm about to ask her this question when I hear a deep, scratchy voice from the backseat say something like, "Yup or Yeah or Yar," I really can't make it out. My neck is still stiff so I have to turn my shoulders and I look in the backseat to discover a third passenger. An older man, probably in his sixties, is making himself at home, eating a bag of popcorn. He smacks his teeth loudly, the teeth he has left, which are stained a purplish-brown. His thin, gray hair shines with grease. The deep wrinkles set into his tan face make his skin resemble a wood carving.

He doesn't actually place the popcorn in his mouth, he tosses it in. Half the kernels miss and land either on his black, sleeveless shirt or all over my car seat. The loose, wrinkly folds of skin on his arms jiggle as he throws the popcorn. He nods at me and says either, "Hey or Ha or Har." I can't understand him. I do notice he's missing his two front teeth and probably several more. How does he chew his popcorn? I sense a unique smell permeating through my car that wasn't there earlier. It has all the subtlety of an overflowing trash dumpster.

I glare at Dylan and she's chewing on another piece of licorice and nodding her head to the music like this situation is completely normal. And safe.

"Did I miss something?" I ask. The song *Jack and Diane* starts up on the radio and Dylan leans forward.

"I love this song," she says and tries to turn up the volume, but I catch her hand in mine. She looks over at me.

"There's a man in my backseat," I point out, trying to stay calm. I pray that Dylan has more sense than to pick up a hitchhiker. Hasn't she ever watched the evening news? More like the evening obituary report? I drop her hand.

"That's Jim," Dylan says as if this should explain everything. "I call him Slim Jim," she adds.

I glance back at Jim and he coughs and it sounds like he's upchucked half a lung into his mouth. He glances around and has the manners not to hock a loogie in my car, so he swallows the mouthful back down. I feel my gag reflex kick in.

"I guess we never went over my car rules," I explain. "See, I have a strict no hitchhiker, or other possible serial killer policy," I say to Dylan.

"Oh, Jim's not a hitchhiker," she says. "I met him at the gas station, while you were asleep. He just needs a lift to New Mexico. He even offered me gas money," she adds.

"So, he's a polite hitchhiker?" I ask. I look around the front seat. "Where's the money?"

She looks at me like I'm rude for asking. "Well, I didn't accept it. Haven't you ever heard the saying, 'Do onto others…?'"

"Have you ever heard of highway safety tips? First being, fasten your seatbelt," I point out, since she forgot to fasten it. She tugs it over her chest and clicks it in place.

"Gray," she says and her voice turns all soft and consoling. "His car broke down and he needs to get back to his family tonight. That's it. You helped me out in Omaha, I'm just passing on the good karma."

I glance back at Jim and he's starting to doze off. His chin is resting on his chest. A white kernel of popcorn is stuck in the corner of his mouth. Low snorts escape his parted lips. He has a dirty black duffel bag on the floor next to his feet.

"He can take a bus," I say and her eyes narrow.

"You're being crabby," she scolds me, like I'm twelve. "You just need some food."

"Crabby?" I say. "My car smells like a urinal. Just pull over at the next exit we come to, Dylan."

"Fine."

Fine. This is Dylan's verbal cue for saying she's mad. *She's* mad? I cross my arms over my chest and strain my eyes out the window looking for an exit, any exit, but we seem to be lost in tumbleweed national park. Then I hear something in the distance. I turn down the stereo and look in the rearview mirror and there's a police car behind us, coming into view over the hill. Blue and red lights rotate and a siren wails.

"I was not speeding," Dylan insists which of course is true. Dylan never drives over fifty-five miles an hour. She's used to handling such clunky, undependable piece of shit cars, she isn't aware that you can actually drive fast in a normally operating vehicle.

She slaps a hand against her forehead. "Is this because I wasn't wearing a seatbelt?" she asks.

Jim's slouching head perks up when he hears the sirens and this time the words that escape his lips are loud and clear.

"Aw, shit," he drawls.

I look over my shoulder. Two police cars are behind us now, sirens on, one in each lane.

Dylan slows down and I hear Jim scuffling in the backseat. I turn and watch him unzip the black duffle bag. He pulls out stacks of cash and starts shoving them under the car seat, the floor boards, anywhere he can hide them.

"Oh, shit!" I yell as I see this happening. Dylan pulls over to the shoulder on the side of the highway and the car kicks up a cloud of dusty brown dirt all around us. I stare behind us in shock as the two cop cars screech to a stop.

Dylan looks over her shoulder as one of the cops gets out of the car and slams the door closed.

"It's a woman," Dylan says and looks at me. "You do all the talking."

"Why me?"

"Bat your eye lashes and finesse her with your smile," she says. "Maybe offer her some free baseball tickets?"

I gawk at Dylan's absurd plan. "You want me to flirt our way out of this?" I look over my shoulder and shudder as she approaches. "I don't flirt with women who flex their muscles while they walk."

Another cop gets out of the driver's seat and raises a loudspeaker in our direction.

"Come out with your hands up," he shouts.

Dylan's eyes widen. I swallow. We watch two more cops step out of the second car. They each rest hands on their gun harnesses.

"They take seatbelt laws very seriously here," Dylan whispers.

I glance over at Jim and he looks frozen to the back seat. It doesn't even look like he's breathing. I wonder if he had a heart attack. Maybe a stroke. A single bead of sweat slides down the side of his face.

"Look in the backseat," I tell Dylan. She glances behind her shoulder and her mouth falls open when she sees stacks of cash wedged under the seat, spilling out. Loose bills litter the floor.

"Oh, crap," she gasps.

"Step out of the car with your hands up," the cop repeats through the loud speaker. "Slowly. No sudden movements. Keep your hands where we can see them."

I inhale a deep breath and open the car door.

Dylan and Jim and I step out, arms raised. Jim's hands are noticeably shaking and the loose skin around his biceps quiver. I'm standing across the car from Dylan, next to Jim and soon three cops are heading our way. They're all wearing silver, reflective sunglasses and they walk as stiffly as robots.

Two of the cops grab onto Jim before he can make a run for the fields. Cars slow down along the highway to watch the arrest. I notice people taking pictures from cameras and cell phones. Excellent.

I set my hands on top of my head as a cop starts to search me.

"Wait," Dylan says across the hood from me. I look over at her. Her eyes are wide with fear as a cop fastens handcuffs around her wrists. For once in her life, Dylan looks scared. I can't wait to hear the words "I WAS WRONG," escape her mouth. I wait for the satisfying sentence to drop.

"I have to tell you something," she says. I stare in her eyes and she doesn't look regretful, or remorseful. It's worse. She looks *guilty*. Her eyes are flooding with guilt. My mouth falls open and I think the worst. She's been on a robbing spree all summer and Jim is her accomplice. She's wanted in eight states for armed theft.

"Nick is gay!" Dylan shouts.

I stare at her across the car as the words sink in. She isn't making any sense.

"What?" I shout back.

"I need you to know the truth, in case we're arrested and I never get to speak to you again." Her eyes are pleading for me not to be upset. It's a little late for that.

"Shut up," one of the cops shouts at us. "You don't speak unless we ask you a question." An officer fastens handcuffs around my wrists. I've always wondered what handcuffs would feel like, but in my mind it is played out in a much kinkier, private situation.

I hear the cop mumbling something to me, but it's inaudible against the thoughts screaming in my head. I blink at Dylan and try to wrap my head around this new piece of knowledge.

"You mean, you're not dating him?" I ask her.

"Nick. Is. Gay," Dylan repeats.

The cop next to me tells us to be quiet. But they could use a stun gun on me and it still wouldn't get my attention.

I glare at Dylan. "As always, your timing is impeccable," I shout at her across the car.

"That's it, split these two up," the female cop shouts. I stare at her massive biceps, stretching her uniform fabric to the point of ripping it apart, and I shut my mouth. The cop next to me grabs me around the back of my neck and nudges me toward his car.

Dylan

"I'm sorry," I say to Gray as I slump into the back of the cop car next to him, behind a mesh of steel wire that divides us from the front seat. I look through the metal bars at all the monitors, lights and keypads. It looks like a time traveling machine. I stare down at my handcuffs. They're heavier than I imagined and just when your hands are confined, your body suddenly starts to itch in the most awkward places.

"Just don't talk to me right now," Gray says as one of the cops shuts my door.

"Okay," I say, a little hurt.

"You're insane!" Gray says to me and my head perks up. I look at him and he's irate and I'm so happy I could scream. I smile at the two glowing words. I'm no longer in a cop car that smells like leather and male deodorant. I'm floating into the sky, rocketing towards the sun, high on Gray's words.

"Don't you dare say thank you," Gray reads my response. "It's not a compliment."

Officer Greg and Officer Bryan (I was polite to use their names during the arrest; good manners will only win you brownie points) get into the front seat and start the engine. We pull off onto the highway.

Gray looks out the window as two detectives pick and prod their way through his car. Jim already confessed I only offered him a ride, and we had nothing to do with the robberies. At least he was a polite felon. But the cops are making us go down to the station as part of the standard investigation procedure.

"How far away is the station?" Gray asks.

"It's in Amarillo," Officer Bryan says. "Enjoy the drive."

"Texas?" I say with excitement. I close my mouth. Tight. I've always wanted to go to Texas, but now probably isn't the time to point out that my favorite part of road trips are the unexpected detours.

Gray mutters out a sigh. He sinks his head back against the car seat and closes his eyes.

***

Two hours later we're sitting in the Amarillo Police Department, across a wide metal desk from the two police officers. Officer Greg is filling out paperwork and talking on the phone, while Officer Bryan seems to be in charge of babysitting us. They look like they could be brothers—both with blues eyes and light blond hair that's buzzed close to their heads. They're taping our cell phones, emails, and bank accounts for any final traces that we could be linked to the robberies. I'm fascinated by the entire procedure and I end up asking the cops more questions than they ask us.

"You're the only person I've ever met who enjoys being investigated," Officer Bryan tells me. "Usually people clam up and want to get out of here as fast as they can." I glance over at Gray and he shakes his head. He only talks when someone addresses him.

Officer Bryan looks over my camera, which ends up being our best witness, since it documents everywhere we've been for the last twenty-four hours. They called Sue Anne and Chris to back up our statements. Once we're cleared from the case, Officer Bryan starts commenting on my photography which turns into a lengthy discussion about tornadoes. He smiles and tells me I should come out storm chasing with him some time.

I look over at Gray and he's reading a magazine. Most of the anger in his eyes has vanished. He looks bored more than anything.

"You each can make a phone call if you want," Officer Bryan tells us. "You won't get your cell phones back for a while, but you can use an office phone."

Gray nods for me to go first. I stand up and follow Officer Bryan into a side office. He introduces me to Debra, the administrative assistant. I sit across from her desk and she picks up the receiver and asks for a number.

I should call my parents, but they're worried enough about Serena. I don't want to give my mom a nervous breakdown. I ask Debra to dial Nick's number and she hands me the receiver. Nick answers before it even rings.

"Hey! How's the sex?" he asks.

I groan into the receiver. "Nick, we haven't had sex. Not even close."

I glance at Debra and she raises her eyebrows, but she keeps her eyes on her desk.

"What? Well *that* is your problem, Dylan. Any other trifling matter you're calling me about is not important."

I look at the legal file that Debra is studying, opened up to a mug shot.

"Okay," I say.

"Have sex with him. Tonight. Make a sex kabob out of that boy, Dylan. Eat him up. Got it?"

"Nick—"

"That's all that matters. And don't you dare call me back until you have something interesting to say. I want some steamy details. Not cable TV Hallmark fluff, I want skin-a-max dirty shit. Bye."

I hear his phone cut off. "Nick. Nick?!"

I hand Debra the receiver and she sets it back on the phone base. There's a wry grin on her face. I start to smile. Sex kabob. I like the sound of that.

Gray

When Dylan walks back in the room, Officer Best Friend Bryan offers to give her a tour of the police station and the jail in the back. Dylan asks me to come, but I decline the sight-seeing experience. I watch them leave and I swear the man is hitting on her. I saw him checking her out when she stood up to use the phone. He even agreed to order a couple of pizzas to the station for dinner. But how often do these guys get tall girls with cut-off shorts in here? They've been treating Dylan like a celebrity guest, not a robbery suspect. Men are so simple. Show them a little skin and they become floor mats.

A few hours ago I probably wouldn't have cared, but a new piece of information is making me care.

Dylan is single.

I look at the cop sitting across from me.

"Can I make a phone call?" I ask. He nods without looking up from his paperwork. I walk in the side office and a name plate on the edge of the desk reads Debra. She looks up and smiles at me. I sit down across from her and give her the number for Lenny, my best friend in New Mexico. We're each other's emergency contacts in college, so I memorized her phone number. Debra hands me the receiver when it starts to ring.

Lenny picks up.

"Hey, Lenny," I say.

"Gray? Hey stranger."

"Stranger?" I mock. "Says the girl who never returned a single one of my texts this summer."

"You know I hate texting."

"You hate anything that's popular," I remind her.

"That's because anything adopted by the masses is usually annoying, since the vast majority of people are annoying. I don't even like recycling."

I smile into the phone, despite my situation. I've missed Lenny's eternal pessimism.

"Lenny, I'm in trouble."

"What is it?" she almost sounds like she cares. "Muscle sprain?" Lenny makes it a priority to give me crap on a daily basis for being a college athlete. She thinks sports are as necessary and helpful to society as fad diets.

"I ran into Dylan a few days ago," I say. I expect to hear a sympathetic gasp on the other end.

"Really? That's great," she says.

I frown.

"No, it's not. She's my terminator. It's like she has some mission programmed in her brain to search out and destroy me. She is what I need to run from, right?"

There's a short pause. "I don't do science fiction references, Gray. What are you trying to say? Are you still in love with her?"

I look around the police station. I mentally recap the last twenty four hours of my life.

"She annoys me more than ever," I say.

"So, you're more in love with her than ever?" Lenny guesses.

I run my hand through my hair.

"Exactly," I admit.

"Then what's the problem?"

"The problem?" I ask. "Should we revisit the last three years, and do you want to ask me that question again?"

"Gray, I don't have the time for your one-hundred-and-one relationship theories."

"Hey, I don't—"

"If you love her, there's only one thing to do," she interrupts me.

"Avoid her?" I say.

"Tell her!" Lenny says. "I always told you, you two are meant for each other. No offense, but shutting her out of your life last summer was a stupid choice."

I blow out an aggravated sigh in response.

"Ask Dylan how she feels. She's always honest," Lenny says. "Maybe she has a plan."

"Dylan doesn't make plans. She unmakes plans. She has planaphobia. The fear of plans."

"Maybe she overcame this fear. Maybe Dylan grew up."

I laugh out loud at this broad misfire. "Very unlikely," I say.

"Sometimes you have to have your heart beaten down before you wise up," Lenny says. "It sucks but it's true. It's the only way we learn anything. She broke your heart and then you broke hers. The score's tied. It's time for a rematch. How do you like my sports reference?"

"Thanks for dumbing it down so the stupid jock can understand," I say.

"I try."

The police officer holds up two fingers to tell me my phone time is almost up. I want to strangle the receiver cord. I feel like Lenny's taking Dylan's side. It's friendship adultery.

"Is this the Shitty Help Hotline?" I ask. "Sorry, I must have dialed the wrong number. I'm looking for Lenny."

She ignores my insult. "Gray, listen to me. There's only one thing you need to ask yourself: Who do you love? That is the most important question you will ever answer in your life."

Only one image comes to my mind.

"I love Dylan."

"Then tell her. I gotta go. I just got to work and I need to shut my phone off."

I say goodbye and I'm not sure if Lenny helped me out or made me feel worse. I bounce her advice around in my head, like a racket ball, hitting it away only to have it slam back again from another direction.

I walk into the main office and Dylan is eating some pizza and talking to Officer Dumb Shit Bryan. Her feet are propped up on a plastic desk chair next to him. His elbow is on the table and he's leaning forward as he talks to her like they're close friends. I sit down across the table from her and the smell of cheese and pepperoni reminds me I'm starving. Three pizzas are spread out on the long office table and I help myself to a few slices and a can of Diet Pepsi.

"I'm just confused," Officer Bryan says. "I really like this girl. We went out on three dates and now she won't return my calls." I stare at Dumb Shit. He's asking for dating advice from the queen of relationship disaster? I stuff my mouth full of pizza before I make a wise crack.

Dylan looks thoughtful and she sets her pizza down on the paper plate. She gives the conversation her full attention. "That's your problem," she says. "Dating."

I want to say that maybe his problem is living in a town with more prairie dogs per capita than women.

"What do you mean?" he asks.

"Dates are the problem," she says. "You should never go on dates. You don't learn anything real about anyone." She licks grease off of her fingers. "Dates are a scam. Most of my friends use them to go to restaurants or concerts they can't afford," Dylan says.

The cop looks over at me and I shrug.

"How do you get to know someone without dating?" he wonders. Officer Greg sits down, helping himself to some pizza.

"People are a lot like places," Dylan says. "Think of it as traveling. When I traveled in Europe, my favorite places to visit were the small towns. I loved Paris and Rome and all the famous cities, but when I was in a small town, I felt like I was starting to understand the country. It's the same thing with people."

He thinks about this. "So how do you hit local spots with a person?"

Dylan shrugs. "Figure out what they do by themselves. Where do they like to go off-roading? Do they read, cook, run, paint, watch movies? Figure out a way to do those things with them. Just stop dating. That is the secret to dating."

The cops stare at her with these enamored expressions. I'm waiting for them to exchange phone numbers. I shake my head and grab another helping of pizza.

Dylan

I walk outside of the police station three hours later, after the authorities were satisfied I was only guilty of stupidly (yet, thoughtfully) picking up a wanted felon (a stranded man in need of help). It turns out Jim robbed three gas stations in Texas. His last robbery was in Kansas, the night before we picked him up.

I stand in front of the entrance of the police department and look up at the purple-blue sky. Stars are peeking through like pin prick holes in a giant tapestry. The moon is a crescent glow, leaning lazily on its side. I can't help feeling sorry for Jim, that he won't see a brilliant sky like this for years.

I hear the door open behind me and Gray walks out. He stops next to me on the stairs and I open my mouth to say something but he holds up his hand. His fingers almost touch my lips.

"Dylan, could you just not for a second?"

"Not what?" I ask.

He drops his hand and looks at me. "Not do or say whatever you're thinking of saying or doing? Not act on every crazy impulse that comes into your head? I'm a little burned out right now."

I look down at my feet and nod once.

Gray walks down the steps, passing me. Over the past twenty-four hours I've fallen in love with him all over again and all I've managed to do is nearly get him killed the first night and arrested the next.

He turns back to fire a look at me. "Does this fill your 'Do one random thing,' quota for the year, please, God?" he asks.

I turn and take a picture of the police station sign before I walk down the steps after him. "At least Jim didn't have a gun in the car," I note.

Gray doesn't respond.

"And it was never loaded in any of the robberies," I point out.

"Wow, that's so considerate of him," Gray says. "He's a real humanitarian."

I start to laugh but the heat from Gray's eyes makes me catch myself. I feel like I'm staring at a funnel cloud that could spin and touch down at any moment.

"I feel sorry for him," I say.

"Why?" Gray asks.

"He only stole because he was desperate, because he couldn't see any other way out of his situation. When you don't have hope, I think it makes you crack."

"Leave it to you to be philosophical about this," Gray says and slips his phone in his pocket. "He's messed up, Dylan. People like that belong locked up."

"He's not evil," I say. "He has a good side to him."

"You have way too much of a soft spot for people. An underdog is one thing. A crazy criminal who robs at gunpoint is another."

I nod. "I really learned my lesson today," I say, looking up at the Amarillo Police Station.

"What's that?"

"Never to pick up a hitchhiker." I look at Gray. "In someone *else's* car. It's rude."

He starts to smile. "You do notice the time, right?"

I look down at my cell phone and feel a frown setting in. "We're never going to make it to Flagstaff."

Gray shakes his head. "Your little detour put us back a few hours," he says and looks at me. "Didn't you say Mike was playing a few shows?"

I nod. "They're supposed to be there for the next two nights."

Gray turns and looks at his car, parked along the curb down the street.

"We'll catch them tomorrow," he says.

I look at Gray and dare to ask. "You're still going to give me a ride to Flagstaff?"

He nearly laughs at the doubt in my voice. "I'm not going to abandon you in Amarillo. Although I'm sure Officer Desperado in there would appreciate it," he says and points his thumb at the police station.

"Hey, look on the bright side. At least we got free pizza out of this," I point out.

This time Gray laughs. It starts out light and then it builds. He laughs so hard he has to sit down on the steps. I start to laugh, too, but mostly I'm just watching him laugh. It's my favorite sound. The words *I love you* almost slip out of my mouth but I catch them on my tongue and hold them in. It feels as unnatural as holding my breath.

Gray looks up at the darkening sky and his laughing subsides.

"I'm not driving eight hours tonight," he says. "And you are hereby suspended from any driving privileges." He points a finger at me.

I nod and try not to pout. "I guess I deserve that."

Gray

The street's quiet. All I can hear are our shoes brushing against the sidewalk and crickets chirping in the trees. I unlock the car door but I hesitate before I open it. I look down the street. I don't feel like driving. I'm sick of sitting inches away from Dylan, but being cooped up in a hotel room sounds as comfortable as a slow strangulation.

I could try and drive and tune her presence out with music but her energy is louder than any band I can play. Her eyes say more than any lyrics.

Her eyes are what catch me—the way they're always wide and surprised and I'm just lost, looking around, trying to figure out what I'm always missing.

The sky is dark purple and the horizon is etched in neon pink. It gives me an idea. "You have a sleeping bag, right?" I ask Dylan, and she nods.

We get into my car which has the strange smell of cologne mixed with cleaning products as if a businessman just used it to sleep with his housekeeper. At least it doesn't smell like a dumpster anymore. I turn on the overhead light and hand Dylan the road atlas.

"Here, itinerary director," I say. "Find me a campsite."

She takes the map and opens it over her lap. I turn on the engine and roll down the windows. The air is crisp and there's hardly any wind. She points to a spot on the map highlighted with a brown teepee. "Found one. It's about one-quarter of my pinkie finger away," she judges the distance.

I take her hand and measure her finger against the scale at the bottom of the map.

"That's about twenty miles," I say. I drop her hand before my fingers want to naturally curl around hers.

As we drive, Dylan informs me we need to stop at a gas station for camping provisions. She lists all the necessary food items: chocolate, candy, salt.

I want to add condoms to the list, but I kick the thought away. Besides, this is part of my plan. I'm not going to touch Dylan in a campground full of couples and families and kids. I can't rip her clothes off. It's an extra security measure.

Otis Redding serenades us down the highway. *Sitting on the Dock of the Bay* might be the most calming song ever recorded. I mean, it has ocean waves and seagulls whistling in the background. And I still can't unwind. Dylan's bare leg is next to me and it's always been my favorite arm rest while I'm driving. Her skin sings louder than the music. My fingers tighten around the steering wheel.

Dylan is single.

Shit.

I turn up the music and drive and keep my eyes focused on the white highway lines. I try not to think at all, just keep my mind like a dry, barren desert. When we pull up to the campground registration, Dylan pays the $14 site fee. She tells me it's the least she can do. She talks to the ranger about which campsites are the best. They all look the same to me, dotted with trees, lined with picnic tables, fire pits and water faucets.

She buys a bundle of firewood and when she jumps out of the car to get it, it looks like she has springs in her feet. She sees this as a vacation. I see it as a diversion.

Dylan gets back in the car and we loop around the campground. In the center is a community shelter with showers and restrooms. I park under a canopy of green leaves. I dig through my car console and find a lighter and Dylan releases her inner-Girl Scout and makes the fire.

I walk around the campsite, not sure where I am physically or mentally. It's like I'm between places. The air is drier out here. I can breathe easier. I can start to sense the desert. The wide open sky is a celestial light show. It's our own planetarium.

I've decided that love makes people stupid. We never learn from our mistakes. I tried love once and I got burned. I tried it once more, just to see if I got it wrong, if the second time around I would be smarter and stay further away from the flame or carry water to put it out completely. The second time around I crashed to the ground in a smoldering heap.

Yet here I am, at its mercy again and I can thrash and flail and roll around, but I can't put it out. I can't escape its drawing heat.

When I get back to our campsite, Dylan is sitting on a blanket next to the fire, poking it and making it jump and dance. I sit down on the picnic table bench, but the fire is making my skin too hot. I lean back and it doesn't help. My brain is steaming. My body is as dry as firewood and Dylan is the flame.

I stand and back up to see which is disturbing me more, the fire or her presence. I glare at Dylan and bring up the words simmering in my head.

"Nick is gay?"

She looks up at me.

"Why didn't you just tell me the truth, Dylan?" I ask her.

"I never said I was dating him," she corrects me, as if this justifies everything.

"That's no excuse," I say.

"I'm sorry," she says slowly, her voice sincere. "Nick knows all about you. He's seen pictures of you, so when he saw you in the parking lot, he was just trying to be a good friend."

I shake my head. "Nick, the dog whisperer," I smirk. "I really hate him."

She smiles. "He's not even a vet. He still lives in his parent's basement," she admits. "Supposedly he's inventing a board game that's going to revolutionize the gaming industry."

I stare at Dylan with shock.

"I wanted to tell you about Nick," she says. "But seeing you and Rachel together threw me off. I wasn't prepared to see you, and then see you with a girlfriend? It was worse than jealousy. I was crushed."

Rachel? Rachel.

Crap.

In all of the craziness of last few days, I completely forgot about my own lie. I start laughing.

"How is that funny?" she wonders.

I look at the fire and my smile falters. It's my last defensive play and I toss it into the flames. "I'm not dating Rachel."

I look over at Dylan and she's studying me with a frown. I'm surprised to see anger in her eyes, but then I realize she doesn't believe me.

"Get over yourself, Gray. You know, you should carry a sign with you that says 'facetious' on it, so you can hold it up after ninety percent of what you say."

"Rachel. Is not. My girlfriend." I sound it out for her in phonetically perfect English. Dylan's eyes narrow and then they widen and I feel like I'm naked, standing in front of her.

"So it was just casual sex?" she asks.

I throw my hands up in the air. "I never slept with her," I say.

She shakes her finger at me. "Don't you dare use the gay line on me. It's not funny. No way is that girl a lesbian."

"She's not gay. She's completely off limits. First of all, she's still in high school."

Dylan's eyes are suspicious. "She looks way too old to be in high school. She looks like she's at least nineteen. And a half," she adds.

I nod in agreement. "The over application of makeup can do that."

Dylan considers this truth.

"Second of all, she's my coach's daughter," I state.

"Oh," Dylan says and pieces this together. "That was your coach we had dinner with?"

"Yes," I say. "He offered to take me out to eat before I left town. We got pretty close this summer."

She nods slowly. "Well, Rachel has a crush on you. You can't deny that."

"She has a crush on every guy on our team. She doesn't know any better. You were right when you said she wasn't my type. *Horses?* Are you serious?"

Dylan smiles. "You told me once you don't have a type," she reminds me.

I press my gaze on her. "Summer flings are not my type," I say and she nods. That much she can understand. I stare at the fire and listen to the wood crackle and pop. I tunnel my fingers through my hair.

"All I wanted to do was give you a ride to Flagstaff," I say. "That's it. Just one, simple ride. But nothing is ever simple with you, is it Dylan? It all has to be one, big, crazy—"

"Epic adventure?" she finishes and looks over at me. She has the nerve to smile.

"Adventure? I swear you're the only person I've ever met that gets less mature as you get older."

She breathes out a sigh, but she doesn't deny my claim.

"Since I've picked you up, I've almost died in a tornado," I say.

She drops a piece of firewood onto the coals and sits back down on the blanket. "I couldn't control the weather," she argues. "Besides they were only F-2 tornados. I heard somebody mention it at the gas station this morning. That's practically a baby."

"What's an F-2?" I ask.

"A tornado rating," she tells me. "They're categorized by their strength. They start at F-1, and go all the way up to F-7. Well, according to my uncle his farts are strong enough to be considered an F-0. But that's just Wisconsin humor for you."

I blink a few times at her. "Fart jokes?" my voice starts to rise. "After everything that's happened, you're making fart jokes?"

"Anytime is a good time for fart jokes," Dylan argues. "Look at the positive side. At least at the end of day, we have a really amazing story."

I cross my arms over my chest. "Is that really all you care about? Having a story at the end of the day?"

She nods without hesitating. I look over at the fire and we're both quiet for a few seconds.

"You should have told me the truth about Rachel," Dylan speaks up.

"I never lied about it," I point out.

"You indirectly lied," she argues. "That's almost worse than lying because it's premeditated."

"You did the same thing," I say and take a step closer to her. "I was planning on coming clean today, but then we spent all afternoon in police custody since you decided to get us arrested."

"Oh, now you're rehashing the past?" Dylan says, her voice rising. "Unbelievable."

"It just happened an hour ago," I yell back.

"I told you I was sorry," she snaps back. "Besides, don't you have to do jail time to even be considered for professional sports? Having a police record will only make you more credible as an athlete," she says.

I glare at her. "I'm laughing hysterically right now," I say, my mouth tight. She turns and looks back at the fire.

I blow out an aggravated sigh. I'm done with fighting. It doesn't even feel like a fight, more like frustrated foreplay. My instincts are telling me one thing and my brain is telling me another. It's a push and pull game in my mind.

I pace back and forth. The world is spinning. My mind is screaming with all the words I want to say but they're trapped in my throat. YOU'RE PERFECT AND BEAUTIFUL AND ADDICTIVE AND AMAZING AND I CAN'T TURN THIS OFF. I CAN'T ESCAPE YOU. I CAN'T GET OVER YOU. I'M STILL IN LOVE WITH YOU. But I can't say this out loud so I shout the frustrated abridged version instead.

"You're insane!"

Dylan watches me. Her face is calm and there's a trace of a smile on her lips. "I love you too, Gray," she says.

My heart reacts to her words by jabbing against my ribs. "That's not what I said."

"Are you sure?" she asks. "Isn't that what you want to say, and you can't? Isn't that what you're always fighting when we're together?"

"We've been apart for more than a year, and now you're suddenly back in my life for one weekend. You can't say you love me," I argue.

She studies my face carefully. "I know you better than anyone. I can tell by the way your lips are tightening up and your eyes are narrowing that you know I'm right and it's pissing you off."

The firelight is doing strange things with her face. Especially her eyes. I can't read what she's thinking. I look at her and suddenly I believe in something. I feel like I'm looking at Fate and Timing and Luck all moving into one tangible space.

I head towards her and get down on my knees in front of her. Everything feels like slow motion. Even my heartbeat is pausing for breath. Movement has new meaning, every touch has complexity. Nothing is easy and it's too easy.

I push her down on the ground and lie over her. My face is inches from hers. I can feel her chest rising against mine. I can smell her smoky hair and skin.

"This is when you should stop me," I warn her.

She answers me by leaning forward and pulling my neck down closer. My lips crash into hers and my body follows and then my heart. I pin her body to the ground and my mouth makes up for a lack of words. It spills out all the truth.

I lean away and take a deep, shaky breath and go back for more. Our tongues collide and I want to pull away but I can't. Her mouth is a high and it's getting me off.

She pulls her hands around my neck and my hand moves across her chest and down to her waist. Her hands move inside my shirt and slowly work their way down and play at the waistband of my shorts.

She's sucking on my bottom lip and I run my tongue over her top lip as if we've been starving for each other. My fingers slowly trace along her jaw and up to her cheek and back down again to her chin. I've been waiting so long just to touch her face.

I'm breathing harder and I run my hand over her chest and push my way under her t-shirt but I can't get enough of her skin so I start to lift it over her chest. I move my arm around her back to unfasten her bra and she reaches her hand all the way down my shorts, under my boxers, and I gasp.

We suddenly hear gravel crunching in the distance. Dylan tugs her shirt down and I glance up to see a couple walking by our campsite. A flashlight beam is guiding their way.

I dip my head down to Dylan's neck and press my lips into her skin.

"So much for your lousy avoidance plans," Dylan says, her breaths deep. She always reads my mind. She bites on the bottom of my ear and it makes me groan with frustration.

"I don't know why I bother," I say, my voice gruff, my heart slamming against my ribs. It doesn't matter. Hands can still go places that eyes can't. I press my mouth against hers and her teeth lightly graze my tongue and I'm lost in her crazy world full of twisting paths. It's my favorite journey.

***

It's hours later and I'm still awake, looking up at a ceiling of stars. Dylan is wearing my hooded sweatshirt and she's curled up in a ball next to me. Her head is on my chest and my arm is around her shoulder. The air is cold; it carries faint traces of fall. A whisper of sunlight edges into the sky. I can almost feel the earth spinning on its axis, always looking for the sun, attracted by her golden light. I close my eyes.

Tonight it was all so simple. The dark is like fuel for desire, always pushing you one step further, encouraging you to take chances while no one is watching. But the light is a harsh judge of night's impulsive decisions. Now everything is complicated. And worse, possibly all a mistake.

My eyes are heavy and dry and they burn from two nights of no sleep. I feel her now, like a ticking clock next to me, reminding me to savor each second, as if my relationship with her is always set on a timer about to go off.

Dylan

Gray slides inside a booth and I scoot in next to him and finally it feels natural between us. My knee pushes against his and I can feel the edge of his sandal press against mine under the table and our arms touch on top of the table. I don't notice the diner or the people, I'm still remembering how last night his hair smelled like smoke from the campfire, how his lips were warm and soft, how salty his skin tasted. I appreciated the camping idea but the only scenery I want to enjoy right now is his naked body. It was so unnerving to be able to feel everything last night and not be able to see anything. I'm a sex-with-the-lights-on kind of girl. Tonight we are getting a hotel room.

A waiter sets down a coffee next to Gray and lemonade in front of me. He slides a plate with a cinnamon roll in between us. I haven't even looked at the menu—I'm not hungry. Love is a powerful appetite suppressant.

I look at Gray's eyes and notice the purple shadows under his lower lids. It strangely brings out their blue color. He changed into a black t-shirt at the campground after he took a shower. It's worn-in and soft and ripping along the hem. He's wearing olive green shorts that hang low on his hips, and flip flops with a Nike swoosh across the top.

"You didn't sleep last night," I say. I touch his cheekbone and graze my fingers over his lips before I pull away.

He shakes his head. "No," he says. "And these diner coffees are a tease. It's like drinking strong water." He dumps a spoonful of sugar in the mug and a creamer. He looks at me. "My brain turns on at night," he says. "I think it's nocturnal."

I nod. "And a sleeping bag spread over rocky gravel is a harder mattress than you're used to." He stirs his coffee.

"I'd do it over again a million times, Dylan," is all he says. His lazy eyes settle on mine. I realize he isn't complaining about last night.

"Does anything help?" I ask.

"I slept really well the summer I met you," he tells me.

I think about our daily hiking trips. "All the exercise?" I figure.

"If by exercise you mean sex, then yes, it was all the exercise."

I nod at the memory. I think we set some world records that summer.

"If scientists could somehow capture the hormones released right after sex, and bottle it as a drug, they would make billions of dollars," Gray tells me. "That is the calmest feeling in the world."

I think about this. "You mean like a liquid gel orgasm capsule?" I ask. I'm trying to picture it. It would definitely have to be a red pill. Candy coated. Cinnamon flavored.

Gray shakes his head. "No, it can't be as potent as an actual orgasm. People would never sleep. They'd be kicking and screaming themselves hoarse."

I nod. "That would definitely be a side effect," I agree. "But a great calorie burner."

"I mean the feeling you get about ten seconds after sex, that floating, perfect, sated feeling."

"Ah-em," Gray and I look up when someone clears their throat and the waiter is standing at the edge of the table, staring at us. He's young and his face is either red from a sunburn or a deep blush. "You ready to order?" he mumbles.

"I think we're good, thanks," Gray tells him. The waiter looks at Gray and nods and scurries away like a mouse diving for the nearest hole in the wall.

Gray wraps his fingers around mine. He looks at my lemonade.

"How can you drink that in the morning?" he asks me. "It doesn't have any caffeine."

I shrug. "It's the happiest beverage." I point at his coffee mug. "Why are so many beverages brown?" I wonder. "Coffee, most sodas, beer, apple cider? It's kind of depressing if you think about it, all the brown things we drink."

He takes a sip of his coffee and stares at me, expressionless.

"Why are you like you?" he asks.

"What do you mean?" I stir the ice around my cup with a straw.

"Did something happen to you? Seriously, where do you get all your optimism from?"

I peel off a layer of the cinnamon roll. "I overcame a traumatic obstacle in my past that turned me into a compassionate, self- actualized person," I state. I stick the cinnamon bread in my mouth and Gray is frowning with disbelief. I take a sip of lemonade.

"Nothing happened to me," I say. "Sorry to be anticlimactic. Does some catastrophic event need to happen in our lives in order for us to appreciate anything?"

"Usually," he nods.

"Well, I want to be optimistic, because I can be. Complaining is such a waste of time. Instead of focusing on what goes wrong, focus on what's going right. It's that simple."

He shrugs. "Good point," he says.

"My mom used to host a women's support club at our house every week."

"That sounds awful," he says.

I smile. "It was," I admit. "But it didn't have to be. It was supposed to an uplifting support group. But it was a two hour window of whining and complaining. They called themselves the Good News Club and it was all bad news. My sister and I would sit in the stairwell and listen and I always thought, that's what I *don't* want. That is the way I never want to live. We voluntarily make choices every day. We choose what we do. We choose who we're with. But people act like it's some kind of a trap. It never made sense to me."

"Then how do you block out all the negative thoughts?" Gray asks me.

"I guess I've mastered the art of daydreaming," I say.

He takes a bite of the cinnamon roll and he licks sugar off his fingers.

"How do *you* escape?" I ask him.

"I can't," he says. "I don't have your amazing talent for lack of attention," he says and follows up with one of his slow smiles.

"You can do better than that," I tell him.

"When I'm bored, I think of conspiracy theories," he says.

I take a long sip of lemonade. "What is it with you and aliens all of a sudden?"

"It's not just aliens," he says. "It's government conspiracies. It's unexplained phenomenons. A kid on my baseball team in high school was obsessed with conspiracies. It's all he talked about. You have a lot of time to kill in the dugout, especially when you only pitch every third game," he points out.

"For example?" I ask.

He points out the window. "For example did you know the government can control the weather?"

I look out at the blue sky. "What? Is that true?"

"It's a theory. That's one thing that explains climate change. The government can make clouds."

He points out white, narrow streaks of clouds stretched behind jets.

"What do you think those streaks are?"

"They're called contrails," I say. "It's short for condensation trails."

"Wow," Gray says, impressed. "It's incredibly hot that you know that."

I shrug. "My dad told me. I was always convinced they were ice highways in the sky, perfect for sledding. He had to ruin my fantasy."

"What if they're not contrails? What if that's just what the government wants you to think? Maybe it's soap," he says.

"Soap?" I look up at the white clouds impossibly high and try to imagine flecks of soap inside of them.

"Supposedly, jets fly around spraying soap all over the sky," he says.

"Why? To wash the sky? What, does it clean up the acid rain?"

He smiles. "That's a good theory," he says. "The soap helps absorb some of the sun's rays and it keeps the earth cooler."

I look back at him, fascinated.

Gray laughs. "I'm not saying I believe any of it," he says. "It's just my distraction."

"Wow. You've opened me up to a whole new world of thought."

Gray rolls his eyes. "Great."

Dylan

Gray hands me his car keys after I take a solemn oath that I will never again offer someone a ride without his authorized and signed approval. I unlock the front door and he walks around to the passenger side.

"What if it's a woman in labor?" I ask across the car from him.

"Definitely no," he says. "I don't want afterbirth all over my backseat."

"What if someone's been shot and they're rapidly losing blood and need to get to a hospital?"

"Same rule applies," he says. I frown at him for his lack of sympathy. "That's what an ambulance is for," he argues.

We both slide into the front seat and shut the doors. I turn on the engine.

"What if it's an abandoned child under the age of five?" I ask.

He shakes his head and I only have one more question.

"Do animals count?" I ask.

Instead of answering me, he shuts me up by leaning over and kissing me. All my thoughts evaporate at the touch of his lips. It starts off slow and soft, but then his lips press harder against mine and his mouth opens up and our breaths combine. His hand squeezes my thigh, and I wrap my hand around the back of his neck because I need him to come closer, but the console divides us. I murmur the words "hotel room" against his mouth because I'm not thinking anymore, just feeling, and Gray leans away. I lean after him, my lips craving more.

"Later," he says. His determined eyes back up the promise. I reluctantly nod. I know we need to get on the road.

Gray tugs a sweatshirt on and lifts the hood around his face. By the time we hit the highway ramp, he's already nodding off to sleep.

***

Flagstaff, Arizona. I see a sign off the highway that we're entering the city limits. The road continues to climb up the mountain to the town hovering over 7,000 feet in the sky. Scrubby bushes and golden desert hills disappear and give way to thick pine trees and lush green forest. It's as if nature is performing a dress up runway show, trying on different fabrics and styles, and we're the audience.

When we exit into Flagstaff, Gray is awake, looking for directions to the comedy club. He directs me through campus and downtown. The old buildings have a dilapidated charm.

We slow down across from a small theater on the main street of town, squeezed between college bars and restaurants. An old marquee over the theater entrance advertises the comedy show starting tonight at 8:00. I look at the clock on the dashboard. It's almost 7:30.

Gray opens the door for me and we walk inside a dim lobby with red velvet walls. A box office desk is in the back corner, surrounded by glass like an old fashioned movie cinema. We stand in line behind a few people, all college-age kids in shorts and sandals and t-shirts, tan from enjoying the last warm summer days.

"Just out of curiosity," Gray asks, "when's the last time you saw Serena?" It takes me a few seconds to remember.

"Easter," I say.

"When's the last time you spoke to her?"

"A couple of months ago," I say. "I tried calling her this summer but she never called me back." Gray looks a little unsettled at this news.

When we're next in line I lean close to the glass partition. "We're here to talk to Mike Stone," I say. "He's performing tonight."

"Really?" the guy selling tickets looks back at me like I think he's stupid. "Thanks for letting me know that, I never would have figured it out."

Haha. Sarcasm at a comedy club. So fitting.

"Sorry. Listen, I've traveled over 2,000 miles for this moment. I've endured natural disasters, detours, even being detained by police officers. I need to see him right now. My future depends on it." I close my mouth and realize I sound like a long distance groupie, the crazy stalker kind that carries ropes and knives, and this worker appears to register the same thing, since he leans back away from the glass.

"You can't talk to the comedians before the show," he tells me.

I open my mouth to argue and he cuts me off.

"Sorry," he says. "The same rule applies to crazy stalkers."

Gray interrupts us and asks to buy two tickets. He slaps down two twenty dollar bills and we get red ticket stubs in return. Gray pulls me away from the partition before security comes after us.

I follow him down the hallway toward the theater.

"I can't believe you actually paid to see the vile Impregnator," I tell him.

"At least it got us inside," Gray says. "I don't think your tactic was working any better."

"I was just being honest," I say.

He grins at me over his shoulder. "I think gauche is the word you're looking for."

"Show off," I say.

He grabs my hand and pulls back a black curtain. We walk into a small, dark theater with a black stage framed with more black curtains. It smells dank and musty. There isn't a single window in the room. Black floor tiles shine under our feet. Even the tables and chairs are black. I feel like I'm standing in the waiting room of death.

"This is a comedy show, right?" I ask, looking around.

There's a bar at the back of the theater, lit up around the sides with ribbons of fluorescent lights. Gray walks up to the bartender who's dressed in a black shirt and slacks. He sets cash down on the counter.

"Where's the green room?" Gray asks the bartender.

He looks at the cash and back at Gray. "Why do you want to know?"

"We have to talk to Mike Stone's girlfriend, Serena," Gray says and points at me. "This is her sister."

"The pregnant one?" the bartender says with a knowing nod.

"She could go into labor any second," I warn him. "You could say we're her ER team."

The bartender grabs the cash and nods to a door behind the bar. "Go for it," he says and pockets the cash.

Gray

Before Dylan opens the door, I get around her and block her way. She looks up at me and her eyes are confused. I know she wants to go flying through the door and jump into her sister's open arms. She probably thinks Serena will cry with happiness and they'll leave hand-in-hand, skipping away together under the starlight. I know how her daydreaming mind works. But I'm the practical one.

"Wait," I say. "Has it occurred to you Serena probably won't be happy to see you right now?"

She blinks up at me but her mind isn't registering the warning. "No," she says. "We're family."

"Yeah, and people can really hate their families sometimes. Most domestic violence is family related," I say. "Even homicides."

"Gray, can we earmark this conversation because it's fascinating, but now is not the time." She pushes me away.

I reluctantly step back and Dylan opens the door. Serena is standing directly across the room from us, in front of a green velvet couch. I only assume its Serena since it looks like a balloon is stuffed under her black sweater. She looks nothing like Dylan, other than being tall. Her hair is as black as crow feathers. Her skin is ivory white and smooth. I can't see a single freckle. Her dark brown eyes widen in surprise and her mouth drops open when she sees Dylan.

"What are you doing here?" Serena asks.

A guy standing next to Serena turns around to look at us and I can only assume it's Mike. He's different than I imagined. He looks like a hipster-nerd, with shaggy hair spilling into his eyes and his jeans fit tighter than any man's should legally be allowed.

I shut the door and stand next to Dylan, assuming my best body guard pose.

"I came to talk to you," Dylan says. She takes a step forward but then she hesitates.

Serena stays planted in place. She covers her arms over her chest and they rest on the bulge of her stomach. There's a coffee table between us, littered with open pizza boxes and cans of Coke.

"Oh, so now you take a sudden interest in my life?" Serena asks Dylan.

"What's up, I'm Mike," Mike says and crosses the room toward us. He extends his hand and Dylan keeps hers pressed to her side. I offer my hand instead.

"I'm Gray," I say. He gives my hand a confident shake and his brown eyes have a clever edge to them.

"Gray," Mike says. "So, your mom was depressed when you were born?"

Dylan puts her hands on her hips. "He's named after the coast of Oregon," she states.

"Oh, I see," Mike says. "So, your mom was stoned when you were born?"

I start to smile, but then I look at Dylan's expression and cough into my hand. It's been a while since anyone's made fun of my name.

"Gray?" Serena says, and her eyes widen. "Wait, you're *Gray*?"

I nod and she eyes me up and down.

"You're a lot hotter than Dylan described," she says. "No wonder she traded in her v-card for you."

I raise a single eyebrow. And we were smart enough to use birth control, I want to add. My wiser half tells me the joke could dangerously backfire right now.

Serena's eyes snap over to Dylan.

"What's going on? What is he doing here?"

"We ran into each other in Nebraska," Dylan says.

"You were in Nebraska?" Serena asks.

"Yes. I've been driving across the entire country trying to find you. To talk some sense into you." Dylan pauses, probably waiting for Serena to thank her and offer her the hug she's been waiting for. Serena only glares at her from head to foot.

"You prance in here with your skinny little waistline and perky boobs to tell me what to do with my life?"

"Um. Not exactly," Dylan says. Her hands start to fidget at her sides.

"Oh, ow." Serena half squats, half falls down onto the couch.

"Are you having a contraction?" Dylan asks and runs up next to her. She sits down at her side and reaches out for her hand but Serena pulls it back.

She shakes her head and winces. "It's just kicking my spine at the moment."

"What if you went into labor?" Dylan asks. "Do you have a birthing plan?" She looks at Serena. Serena looks at Mike. Mike looks at me, as if I have any input.

"How hard can it be?" Serena says. "Women have been delivering babies for centuries. It's what we're biologically designed to do. Our bodies haven't changed. Women used to do it in caves next to fire pits and bite on sticks."

"What are you saying?" Dylan asks. "You want to perform a cave birth?"

"That would be awesome," Mike adds. "We can start a new birthing trend. Cavernous births. Slip out of one cave and into another. Talk about a natural transition."

Serena winces again. "I swear he's kicking my throat." She massages her stomach. "Simmer down, Luke."

"Luke?" Dylan asks, her voice rising in excitement. "You're having a boy?"

Serena nods. "Despite the rumors, I *have* seen a doctor."

"Well, as long as you don't name your daughter Leia, then it's alright with me," Dylan jokes. Backfire. Serena's eyes fill with a surge of rage. I'm waiting for fire to blow out of her mouth.

"You haven't spoken to me in months and you walk in here and critique the name of my kid?"

"I was just jok—"

"Do you know the hellish torture that pregnancy is?" Serena cries. "Did you know that your feet and your ears and your nose grow? Did you know you get moles?"

"You look amazing," Dylan tells her and places a hand on her arm. "You're seriously glowing."

"Oh, fuck you," Serena replies. She lays her head back against the couch and groans.

I bite my lips together. Okay, no jokes and no compliments. Maybe Dylan should have researched how to handle hormonally unstable pregnant women before she entered into this conversation. Maybe the trick is no talking at all.

Dylan looks over at me with surprise, as if some alien being has entered her sister's body and she doesn't recognize her anymore.

Mike senses the problem.

"Here's the trick to talking to a pregnant woman," he offers and we all turn to look at him. "It's a lot like talking to a sea animal. They don't really understand what you're saying, but they respond well to hand gestures and food. I carry powdered sugar donut holes with me at all times and toss them at Serena to reinforce positive behavior. It works really well." He nods at the coffee table. "Cheetos would probably work, too."

Serena tries to get up but she's wedged to the couch. She points in our direction. "That is it. GET OUT!" she screams.

I willingly take the exit cue and follow Mike outside.

"Can I buy you a beer?" he asks me as the door closes behind us, and I nod.

"Definitely," I say.

Dylan

I turn back to Serena. She has some rage to spill, and I'm going to stand here and take the assault. I'm the target and she's throwing the darts. Here we go.

"What are you doing here, Dylan?" she asks. "Are you here to make me feel even fatter?"

"I'm worried about you," I tell her truthfully.

"Why? You've never worried about me before."

"That's not true," I tell her.

"You don't know anything about me," she says. "You left home years ago and hardly looked back. You barely talk to Mom and Dad. You hardly ever call. You come back and visit once or twice a year with your scrapbooks and your insane stories and we never know what to believe. You've missed out on a lot."

Her face is hurt and angry and I wish I would have listened to Gray. I should have prepared myself for this.

I raise my arms. There's only one thing to say. "Well, I'm here right now."

Serena runs her hands over her stomach and sniffles. Her mouth starts to tremble. "You don't know what this has been like. Do you know that my bladder is as flat as a pancake because it's smashed under a bowling ball? Do you know that every time I sneeze, I pee myself?"

I shake my head. "I wasn't aware."

"All I can wear are pants with elastic waistbands. Do you know how degrading that is?"

I think about the image. "Actually, that sounds really comfortable."

"Oh, you would say that." She wipes a tear out of the corner of her eye. "What do you want, Dylan?"

"I want you to come home," I say.

She laughs at my suggestion. "Home?" she says. "Where's home? With Mom and Dad?" She shakes her head. "That's not my home anymore. Home is with Mike. I belong with him, I can't just leave him."

"But—"

"What am I supposed to do?" she interrupts me. "Follow your example? Fall in love and then run away and make the guy suffer while I 'figure myself out?' Is that the way it works?"

I shake my head and step around the attack. I don't want to fight with my sister. That's not why I came here. I take a deep breath and sort out my thoughts, choosing my words carefully as if I'm gently poking a fire, trying not to make any sparks fly.

"You know I love you Serena, even if we haven't been living in the same house the last few years. A lot of people leave after high school. Most people move away or go to college. It doesn't mean I don't care about you guys. It doesn't mean I don't think about you and Mom and Dad all the time and carry you with me everywhere I go."

"I know," she says. "And I've always respected you for leaving. I've always looked up to you."

"You? Looked up to me?" I ask.

"Of course I did. A lot of people say they're going do these crazy, wild things. But hardly anyone does. You follow through with everything you say you're going to do. You never let anyone try to hold you back." She meets my eyes. "But then let me do the same thing. You're not the only one who wants to be independent."

"It's different, Serena," I say gently. I pick up a bag of Cheetos on the table and hand her a few. She accepts them, swallows a mouthful and then grabs the bag from me and digs her hand inside. Her eyes lose a little of their guarded hostility. Maybe Mike was right.

"I didn't have another life depending on me," I say. "Sure, I was independent, but I also wasn't nine months pregnant driving around the country."

Serena looks down at her basketball-sized stomach.

"Do you have any idea what you're going to do when he's born? You're going to need a doctor. You're going to need to stay put for a while. Let me help you get settled."

Serena stares at the wall in front of us. Her lips are tight.

"I know what I'm doing."

That's not the point I'm trying to make. I choose my next words carefully. "You need to think about Luke. This isn't just about you anymore. Please don't be selfish about this."

She looks over at me. "You should talk. What about Gray?"

"What about him?"

"You've never considered Gray. Yes, I have a baby to consider, so it's not just about me. But a relationship is the same thing. It shouldn't have to take having a baby to understand that it's not all about you."

I narrow my eyes.

"You're right," I admit.

"So don't call me selfish, Dylan. I'm actually trying to make this work with Mike because I love him. We're figuring it out. I didn't want to stay home and have Mom and Dad tell me how to raise my kid. I don't like being told what to do either."

"But you're going to need help, Serena. Just let us help you."

She shakes her head. "I don't want your help."

My stomach starts to knot. "So, that's it?" I ask. "What about Mom? Would you let her fly out here?"

She looks down at her feet.

"Whenever I have a problem Mom just hounds me. She tells me what to do. She'll make everything worse."

"I'm sorry," I tell her. I'm reaching for anything to make her change her mind. "Maybe it feels like she's smothering you. I guess love does that sometimes. But isn't that better than no support at all?"

Her eyes start to tear up.

"When I'm ready, I'll call you. I promise. When I'm ready. But I don't want you here right now. If you really want to help me, leave me alone." Her stubborn eyes tell me the debate is over.

I breathe out a sigh.

"Fine," I say.

Gray

Dylan silently slides into my car and shuts the door. I climb in and start the ignition. She's scaring me. She hasn't spoken since she walked out of the green room. I can only guess at the verbal shrapnel that's cutting her up inside. I don't want to say the usual stupid catch phrases. *What's wrong? You okay? What can I do? Do you want to talk about it?* So, I just stay silent.

The stereo's loud and I reach over to turn it down and Dylan catches my hand.

"Will you put in some music?" she asks, and I nod. I can always handle the job of musical supervisor. I can sense the feelings flooding her mind and I look through my CD's for something that might help. I slide in an album by The Lumineers.

We drive through downtown Flagstaff, passing historic hotels with brick facades and welcoming green awnings. We're over seven thousand feet high, but I don't think Dylan has ever felt lower.

I keep my eyes alert for the nearest highway sign out of here. I haven't been to Flagstaff in four years. The last time I was here, I was at a hospital with my parents where we found out from a room full of strangers that my sister was dead. And we didn't get there in time to say goodbye. She died before she went into surgery. They warned us before we saw her—she had head wounds from the accident and she wouldn't look the same. I can still see her purple-gray lips and pale skin. I remember how cold the room felt and how I saw black spots behind my eyes before I passed out.

I vowed I would never return to this place again.

My foot pushes down on the accelerator when I see a highway ramp.

I wouldn't have come here for anyone except Dylan. I realize I never stopped loving her. I was in love with her the moment I saw her face in Omaha. Because I didn't say no to her. It's not very often you agree to revisit your demons. People don't normally welcome back their worst nightmares.

My eyes start to blur. I don't even know if I'm entering the right highway. But I need to put some distance between us and this town and the driving helps. It's a small amount of control in this world so out of my control. I like how the highways bend and turn out here. It forces you to focus on driving, not just zone out like you can put life on auto pilot.

While I drive, I watch Dylan out of the corner of my eye. She sits back in the seat and her eyes are locked on some point in the distance. I turn the music up louder and I understand how she feels because I've been there.

I see a motel off the road and I slow down. It's hardly visible behind a thick wall of pine trees. The parking lot is on a narrow side street, and I like that it's hidden. Sometimes, when life slams a door in your face your only defense is to shut it out for a while. Dylan doesn't understand this, her mind doesn't go that dark. She never feels the need to hide, so tonight I can show her how.

I park and look out at the moon and the stars. They glow above us like a chandelier, suspended by invisible chords. I wonder what keeps them from crashing down.

I turn off the motor but the music is still playing around us, surrounding us and we are just surfaces for sound to bounce of off. Dylan shifts in her seat and her eyes look over at me and they focus on mine. I can tell the windstorm in her head is starting to settle.

"Thanks," is all she says.

I get out of the car and walk across the parking lot to the lobby but my mind isn't in my body. It's floating with the starlight, looking down on my precarious situation. My movements are in slow motion, or maybe I'm simply trying to stretch time out and make it last. I know this might be my last night with Dylan.

The hotel manger hands me a room key with a plastic handle. When I find our room, Dylan heads for the bathroom and I bring in our bags. In the side of my duffle bag is a box of condoms I bought at a gas station this morning. I doubt Dylan will be in the mood, but it's better to be safe than, well, in her sister's situation.

I sit on the end of the bed and look around the room. The carpeting is dark green, like seaweed, and the walls are hung with generic ocean prints. I feel like the bed is an anchored ship.

I hear the shower running in the bathroom and I scroll through channels on the TV. I have a feeling

Dylan will want to crash after all the drama today. I hear the water turn off and a few minutes later the door cracks open and a puff of steam lazily spills into the room. Dylan walks out in her bare legs and the green over-sized t-shirt. She's combing her wet hair with a brush she bought earlier today and it falls straight and dark, touching the tops of her shoulders. I look at her legs and her wet shining hair and I remind myself to behave, but the ways she looks at me, like she's looking inside of me, makes it hard.

"Good news." My voice cuts through the thick silence. "*Sleepless in Seattle* is on. Our favorite movie stars."

Dylan doesn't respond. She keeps her eyes on me and narrows them a little.

"Okay, you've said seven words in the last hour," I say. "That's a record for you. And it's really freaking me out."

My eyes follow her as she walks over to the edge of the bed. She stands in front of me and takes the remote out of my hand and turns off the TV with a buzzing snap. My hand still lingers there, hovering in the air, in the space between us. I have strings and they are connected to her hands and she's playing me. And she knows it.

Dylan tosses the remote on the floor and she climbs onto my lap. Her legs straddle my waist. She lifts her shirt over her head and she isn't wearing anything underneath. Her freckled skin glows in the golden light.

I inhale a sharp breath. I look over her body, something I couldn't do last night in the dark. I take my time, drinking in every soft feature. I wrap my hands around her hips and pull her close. She rests her arms on my shoulders and her fingertips feel like tiny bites on my skin.

The only sound in the room is the shower still dripping beads of water onto the linoleum. I can almost hear the steam rolling as I move my hands higher up her waist and all these emotions flood through my head and into my heart and then explode through my veins. Even my eyes hurt, everything hurts because I am holding the only thing I want. I press my lips against hers before I say something stupid, like ask her to marry me, or do something stupid, like cry. My hands are shaking and that's the scary thing about love. It makes you shake.

I decide to stop thinking and let my mind drown in this fucking fragile, volatile thing that is happening between us.

All the blood in my body rushes to one place with so much force it makes me shudder. I push her down on the bed and climb on top of her. I kick off my shorts and shoes without letting go of her lips. I come up for air only to peel off my t-shirt. I reach down to the floor next to the bed and grab the condoms out of my bag.

I rip the wrapper open with my teeth and kiss her while I unwrap it and put it on with one, easy glide. I feel like I'm laying claim over Dylan. Every time I move inside of her I want to say *mine*. You're mine. I'm staking something that has always been mine, that should always be mine. I'm immortal and high and tightening and pulling apart all at the same time. I put my hand between her legs, a trick I learned the first summer we met, and pretty soon her legs are shaking along with mine and her breathing turns into a shudder. I sink into her and hold on.

She pants for air and traces her fingers around my temples and through my hair and I'm pulled apart. I'm done and we're both breathing hard, but I don't pull out. I press all my weight into her and breathe.

"Are you okay?" she asks. I feel her throat move under my mouth.

Yes. No. Perfect. Awful. Fuck me. No pun intended.

I nod and blink against her skin as tears gather in the corner of my eyes and I'm crying. I'm fucking crying. I turn my face into the pillow and squeeze my eyes hard and blink away the tears. I'm afraid to move, afraid I'll fall apart and Dylan doesn't say anything. Her fingers just swirl and move and play. I roll off of her and she rests her head on my chest and after a few minutes she falls asleep on top of me with her arm draped over my shoulder. I stare up at the ceiling and feel like I'm in the middle of nowhere and the center of everything.

Maybe we're just two fucked up souls, lost, only complete when we're together. Maybe that's what love is all about. Being humble enough to admit you can't make it on your own. You need a person in order to call a place home. You need love to save you from yourself. You need to love another person so you give a little something every day.

"Dylan, what are you doing to me?" I mumble to the ceiling.

Dylan

After a three-hour morning sex marathon, we emerge from the hotel room, slow and stiff as if we just ran a triathlon. I have sex hair. Not bed hair—sex hair. It is much more violently rumpled than bed hair. I leave the windows in our room open so it can air out. It smells like latex and sweat inside. I carry out the garbage with me because I'm a little embarrassed there are six used condoms inside. I throw the garbage in a trash can next to a bench outside our hotel door.

Gray opens his trunk and tosses a baseball cap at me. I catch it and examine the black fabric.

"You might want to put it on," he says. "You look like you've been electrocuted." He points to my head.

I smile and tug the cap over my wild hair. He grabs my hand and we walk to the lobby to check out. My legs ache and my thighs hurt and my steps are wobbly.

"Ow," I say. Gray looks over at me. "My crotch is so sore," I moan loudly, just as we realize there's a family walking behind us. We turn and the mother shoots me a slut stare and pushes her two younger boys towards their car.

"Classy," Gray says.

"Sorry, but it's true. Does your penis ever get sore?" I wonder.

"Never," he says without hesitating. "That's like asking somebody if they get sore from an amazing massage. No, they just feel absolutely amazing."

He opens the door for me and we walk inside the lobby. The small room is warm and stuffy. I sit by the window and examine a pile of books stacked on the ledge while Gray checks out. The books are ragged, with torn covers faded from the sun. I pick one up and look at the cover, featuring a picture of the Eiffel Tower. I read words underneath the iron statue. *Je t'aime.*

I stare at the phrase, how simple the words look in another language, how elegant like it's the name of a painting, or a movie, or a song. They're not intimidating. They roll off your tongue. They're something to be celebrated, lyrics to write, poems to recite.

I follow Gray outside and as we cross the parking lot to his car, I start to panic. I was so busy enjoying the beginning of everything, I never prepared for the end. I refuse to accept that this is *it.* I refuse to say my least favorite word of all time: goodbye.

I open up a complimentary state map of Arizona I took from the lobby counter and stare at the interconnecting jumble of lines and highways.

We haven't discussed our next move. We haven't had the "us" talk yet. How have we missed this pivotal conversation? Last night, leaving Flagstaff, there was only one clear thought in my head, and that was Gray. The roads were twisting around us while we drove and I couldn't see beyond each turn. I didn't know where we were going, and I didn't care because I was with the only person I wanted. I look over at Gray as he walks across the parking lot. How do you make a person your final destination?

I stare down at the map of Arizona, desperate to lengthen the moment. We can't separate like this. The end of our road trip was always a vague time, a far away date.

A green space hovers over my finger on the map.

The Grand Canyon. We're practically there. The base of the south rim nearly touches our highway exit.

"Can we go?" I ask Gray.

"You've never been to the Grand Canyon?" he asks and I shake my head. "You're really capable of picking a destination?" he asks, his eyes on mine. I know there's more to his question. The Grand Canyon feels like the perfect place to spill my mind. It might actually be large enough to hold all of my thoughts.

"It would be the perfect ending point to our itinerary," I say.

He smiles. "I can almost hear your camera shaking in your backpack," he says.

***

I'm not prepared for this much beauty. It's like seeing spiritual transcendence fall to the earth and lay down at your feet. Your only instinct is worship it, and be humbled in its presence. Even though the canyon is in front of me, right under my feet, I still think I'm imagining it. There is the past, mixed with the present and suddenly you can see time, the way it gathers in waves of dust and dirt and rock.

I stare out at the sea of rock walls beneath us. Sounds don't have to compete out here, they each get their own solo. A bird crows in the sky, followed by a breeze blowing through the trees. A tourist shouts.

"Can we hike to bottom?" I ask Gray as we sit down at the edge of a trail to take in the view. I wonder if there is a bottom. I would rather imagine it goes on forever, like space, the further you go the more it expands.

"You need to buy a permit to do the hike," Gray says. "They sell out almost a year in advance."

"She's a popular place," I say.

He nods. I want to promise him we'll come back here together. Someday we'll do this hike and we'll sleep 5,000 feet under sea level. I wonder how cold it is, or if the stars look any different. I wonder if you can hear the stomach of the earth rumbling. All I know is I want to experience it with Gray. I don't want this to be our last day together.

We both kick off our shoes and sit at the rim's edge. I take a picture of our naked feet, dangling over the mouth of rocks and set my camera aside. It might be my favorite picture yet. I press my knee against his and let my head rock onto his shoulder.

"You're a lot like this," he says.

"A big empty hole?" I ask. "Thanks."

"Something you can never really understand," he says. "The longer you stare at it, the more complex it gets. The more it just keeps going on and on forever."

"So, it's better just to admire it from a distance?" I figure. Gray smiles.

"Sometimes."

"It must drive you nuts." I wrap my arms around my knees and look down at the chasm. I swallow down a bubble of sadness forming in my throat. I know what he's trying to say. "So you're giving up on me?" I ask. "For good?"

"I'm just accepting it, Dylan. It's who you are."

I nod slowly. "So, I'm the Grand Canyon, to you? Is this your metaphorical way of saying we can never be together? Because no one can ever live in the Grand Canyon. It's a National Park," I point out in case he doesn't know, as if he didn't just pay a twenty-dollar entrance fee to use the parking lot. Gray looks over at me and our eyes lock. His eyes completely match the blue sky around us.

"Am I off limits to you?" I ask.

"You make yourself off limits to people. You push people away, just like I do. You run away before you ever have to feel tied down. You make it impossible for people to get too close to you. The only difference is, you do it by accident. I do it by choice."

I look out at the canyon. She seems so old and wise. I wish she could tell me what to do in this moment. What to say. Every word suddenly feels paramount.

"That's why Serena's mad at you," Gray says.

I lift my shoulders. "I went after her. I tried."

"Dylan, has it ever occurred to you, maybe your sister is just like you?" Gray asks. "Maybe you're not the only free spirit in the family?"

I look at Gray and his eyes are still on me. "I don't know what else to do."

"You have to keep trying," he says. "You have to go after her. You don't give up on your family."

I look away and feel the back of my eyes sting. I know he's right. But a tiny, selfish voice inside of me wants Gray to tell me to give up, to run away with him. To stay with him. It would be easier. It would be an excuse. But Gray knows I need to spread myself out in order to be happy. Gray is the only person who has ever loved me enough to understand. I feel a pang in my chest, something like rejection. He's letting me slip through his fingers again. And this time I didn't want him to let go. But our roads always seem to split into opposite directions

I take a long, concentrated breath. Beginnings are so easy. You are fresh, new, fully charged. It's the closing that is always impossible. We stumble and trip because we are suddenly tied to our actions and they become chain reactions. The last step you take, the last word you say, the final note to a song, the ending to a story. That is when the pressure hits.

"I don't know where she's going now," I say. "Flagstaff was the last show Mike posted on his website."

"You'll figure it out," he says. "You have to."

"Why?" I ask and look at him.

"Because you have a sister," he says. He points behind us. "Mine died in a hospital, in Flagstaff, four years ago and I can never get her back. I know this all seems devastating and tragic to you right now, and I'm not saying what happened with Serena isn't a big deal, but I'm *jealous* of you. Because this is just a fight. You can fix this. You can still have her in your life. That is a privilege. Don't lose that."

I feel tears in my eyes, finally spilling out and it's a relief to let them go. Tears stream down my face and I'm starting to see things clearly, even through my blurry vision.

"I didn't realize how much I loved Amanda, how much I needed her, until she was gone. Don't make that mistake," Gray says.

"I love you so much," I tell him. I wipe my fingers over my wet cheeks to try and dry them off. "I'll always love you. You believe that, right?"

He nods slowly.

"Then what about you?" I ask. "What about us?"

He looks at me. "Was there ever really an *us?*" he asks. "Or just a me, and a you, and these random moments when our lives accidently collide? Maybe that's it for us."

I look out at the canyon and suck in a deep breath. I can't accept this theory. I don't believe in accidents.

"I wasn't just upset about Serena last night," I say. "It was something she said. She told me I drew this out between you and me, for three years, because I was only thinking of myself."

He leans back on his hands. "Don't compare yourself to Serena," he says. "Her situation is completely different. If I knocked you up in Phoenix the summer we met, everything would have changed. You might have even accepted my proposal," he says.

"I think about that sometimes." I look over at Gray. "Was that real? I mean, what would have happened if I had said yes?"

He runs his hand over his hair. "I don't know. I think I would have seriously married you," he says. "I was so crazy about you. You became my entire world that summer."

"I don't think I would have regretted it, like I said I would. Maybe I should have said yes."

"I'm glad you didn't," Gray says.

I exhale with relief. At least he's forgiven me.

"Really?" I ask.

"I don't want to be married in college," he tells me. "And when you left it forced me to stand on my own feet. It took a while, but I finally managed. I think if you had stayed with me, I would have always depended on you, like a crutch. I think that would have pressured you after a while."

"I've been thinking about love," I say. "You know how you always say I throw the word around too easily?"

"Yes. You do," he says.

"Well, I realized something over the past year. You can love anyone. It's not that hard. I love Nick. I love my friends and my family. I love bacon," I say and Gray smiles. "But it's different to be *in* love. I've only ever been in love with you."

Gray doesn't respond. He just looks out at the silent canyon.

I stand up slowly, my body stiff, and take pictures of the canyon walls. I ask Gray to take my picture with the canyon in the background. I hold out my hands to show it off, like it's a new car.

Gray drops the camera and studies me.

"You know why I love you?" he asks and walks up closer to me. "You're this," he says and jostles the camera in his hands. "To me."

"I'm a camera?" I say and he nods. He aims the camera out at the canyon and starts to take pictures.

"Why do you love your camera, Dylan?" he asks.

I sit down and think about it. I could list a million reasons. Gray sits next me. "It helps me to see," I say. "I appreciate so much more when I have it. It widens my perspective; it makes me want to soak up every detail. It never misses a thing, it never blinks. The whole world is crisper and brighter and clearer. It sees beauty without judging it. It makes me want to take every temporary moment and make it permanent."

I stop rambling and look over at Gray. He's smiling. "Exactly," he says.

"I'm your camera," I say, stunned. It's the greatest compliment he could ever give me.

Gray

Dylan's cell phone suddenly rings and she takes it out of her pocket and checks the caller I.D. on the screen. She gasps.

"It's Serena," she says and nerves shoot through my stomach as she accepts the call.

"Hello?" Dylan asks and her eyes instantly widen. I can faintly hear screams coming through the speaker. "Okay, okay, just try to stay calm. Where are you?"

I stare at Dylan and her eyes are absorbed as she listens.

"How much time is there between your contractions?" She nods. "About twenty minutes? And they're light? Okay, you'll be fine. You have plenty of time. You're only an hour from the hospital. Early labor can last all day," Dylan tells her. She rolls her eyes. "No, I haven't had a baby out of wedlock, I just did some research to try and help you."

Dylan's face breaks into a beaming smile.

"You want me there? In Los Angles?" she says. She looks at me and I nod.

"We're on our way." Dylan turns off her phone. "She wants me there!" she shouts.

We both jump to our feet and Dylan turns to the Grand Canyon. "There's going to be a baby!" she screams out. Her voice echoes against the rocks.

Tourists around us clap and offer their congratulations. I grab Dylan's hand and pull her down the trail.

"Sorry," Dylan says. "But you should always shout good news."

We turn and race down the trail for the parking lot and dive into my car. I have the car running before Dylan even shuts her door. My hands are shaking as I shift into reverse. Why am I nervous?

"You ready?" I ask.

Dylan nods and her eyes are focused out the window with determination. She sticks her arm out the open window and slaps the side of my car like it's a horse. "It's game time," she says.

We wind through the park roads and the twenty miles per hour speed limit makes it feel like a slow crawl.

Her cell phone rings again and she looks down at the screen.

"Serena?" I ask and she smiles and shakes her head.

"It's Nick. I know exactly what he wants. I'm putting him on speaker." Dylan accepts the call and holds the phone between us.

"Yes, Nick," Dylan says. "We had sex."

Nick screams so loud in response I'm afraid the phone is going to explode. Dylan muffles the speaker with her hand and we can still hear him cheering. Okay, I'm starting to like Nick.

"We've had so much sex every muscle in my pelvis is sore," Dylan says. Nick hoots in reply.

"That's because you've been straddling a stallion. Oh, honey, I am so happy for you," Nick's voice beams.

I shake my head, but I'm smiling.

"I love you Nick," Dylan says.

"I love you both," Nick sings. "Give Gray a BJ for me," he says before hanging up.

Dylan hangs up and laughs. We leave the edge of the canyon behind and head for the water that receded millions of years ago, emptying into the Pacific Ocean and next to the city where anything is possible: Los Angeles.

PART THREE: FINAL DESTINATION

Gray

Dylan's sister is at a hospital in Santa Monica, an ocean side town that edges the Los Angles metropolis. We park on the side of the street and I get out of the car and notice across from the hospital is a spa, fitness gym and sushi restaurant. I feel like I'm standing next to a cliché.

I look up at the looming entrance and hesitate outside the doors. I hate hospitals. I'm about to offer to wait in the lobby so I can secretly escape outside and avoid the entire scenario, but Dylan is already pulling me through the automatic doors to the registration desk. She gives the receptionist her name and she checks her computer screen and nods.

"Serena listed both of you as visitors," she says. "You can go up to delivery."

"Great!" Dylan beams.

Um, what?

I point to myself. "Me?" I ask and my voice cracks like I'm straining to speak.

The nurse nods. She hands each of us orange wrist tags to put on, for security reasons. Dylan peels the backing off one, grabs my left arm, and sticks it around my wrist. She leaves plenty of room, but it feels too tight.

The nurse points to the elevator next to the check-in desk.

"Fourth floor," she says.

I look up at the ceiling and horrific images of projectile streams of blood and screaming women fill my mind.

"I don't think—"

"My sister must want you there, if she added your name," Dylan interrupts me and takes my hand.

"But—"

"Come on," she says and yanks me inside the elevator.

"Dude, I hardly know your sister," I say as the metal doors slide closed.

"Dude?" Dylan asks. "Is that LA surfer talk?"

"That's me being very uncomfortable talk. Dude, I don't ever want to see your sister's vagina."

Dylan laughs. "You don't have to be in the room with us. You can wait outside the door." She presses four and it lights up. Anxiety escalates inside me as we climb each floor. It's as if we've suddenly gone up four thousand feet in elevation. I'm light headed and dizzy.

The elevator opens and we walk into yet another lobby and stop at another registration desk. A nurse in blue scrubs is sitting behind the counter.

"Dylan and Gray?" she assumes. "Go on in." She points down the hall. "Delivery Room Four."

We walk down the hallway and when we turn the corner, Mike is there, pacing outside the door. He's clutching an icepack to his shoulder.

"She kicked me out!" Mike says helplessly when he sees us. "And she bit me," he adds. He takes the ice pack away to reveal a purple and yellow bruise complete with defined teeth marks. It's impressive. Serena has some nice incisors. "She's calling our baby Satan's Spawn. She's lost it, Dylan. How long has your sister been chemically unbalanced? Is it a family gene?"

I look at Dylan and consider the possibility.

"She's in pain Mike, and she didn't learn any of the coping strategies they teach in this amazing place called a *birthing class*," Dylan tells him.

"Oh. I missed that class. Wait." He pulls out his cell phone. "Thank God for YouTube."

Dylan sighs and grabs my hand but I hold back.

"Shouldn't we put on some scrubs? Or wash our hands? What about those rubber gloves?" I ask.

"This isn't surgery," Dylan says. I reluctantly follow behind her. I see DELIVERY ROOM 4 in white stenciled letters on the door and I hear organ music pounding in my head, low and sinister. I'm expecting to see Serena on the bed with her feet buckled into harnesses. Somebody will be grabbing onto her ankles and a sweaty nurse will be screaming for her to push. A doctor will be yelling, "The baby hasn't turned! I'll have to go in! More hot water, boil water, you fools!" because that constitutes my movie knowledge of childbirths.

When we walk in I'm relieved to see the television is set to a baseball game, and Serena is leaning over a huge medicine ball. Everything is calm until Serena screams like somebody's stabbing a knife in her stomach. I lean back against the door and it closes and I'm trapped.

Dylan is on the floor with Serena, trying to grab her hands. A nurse is bending over her.

"That was a good one!" the nurse exclaims and Serena sits up and gasps for air. The nurse applauds her like physical agony is a wonderful accomplishment. What a horrible person.

"I'm so glad I'm having a boy so he will never have to experience this," Serena moans. "The joy of childbirth my fat ass."

Mike peeks his head in the door and I back away and let him in. Serena whips her head around and glares at him.

"This is your entire fault," she yells at him and she rolls to her feet. I swear sparks are flying out of her eyes. "You did this to me!"

He walks up to her and tries to grab her hands. He looks beaten down, like he's been fighting in a boxing ring for the past six hours.

"I want drugs," Serena cries into his shoulder.

"Okay," Dylan says, her voice soothing, "let's get you some drugs."

"No," Serena wails. "It's bad for the baby."

"Drugs are fine," Dylan says.

Mike nods enthusiastically. "This is LA, they've got to have the best drugs around," he says. We all look at him and he shrugs. "I'm just trying to be supportive," he defends himself.

Dylan walks up to him and I watch her with amazement. I have never seen Dylan look more serious, more focused, more domineering. It's a very sexy look for her.

"If you want to be supportive," Dylan says to him, "then you need to be her coach right now. Walk her through this. Encourage her. When she's having a contraction don't try to make jokes. Just look in her eyes and tell her she's doing a great job."

Mike nods and curls his fingers around Serena's shoulder. "Come on, slugger," he says. "Dig deep and show me what you've got."

I start chuckling and catch myself and cough in my hand. Serena shoves Mike away with her elbow and he falls back onto the couch. He glances at the TV.

"Hey, when did the Cubs score two runs?" he asks.

"That's it, both of you, OUT!" Serena shouts. Mike sprints for the door and I shoot Dylan a sympathetic look before I follow behind him.

Dylan

Serena works through another contraction. Her entire body tenses up and her back curls inward in pain as she takes tiny wisps of breaths. She squeezes my fingers so tightly my joints push together but I don't let go and I don't take my eyes off of hers, which are staring into mine, begging for me to make the pain stop.

After a few seconds she lets out a moan and falls back against the pillows. I brush away sweaty hair from her face and wipe a cool washcloth over her forehead.

A nurse comes in and checks her over. She pulls a blanket over Serena's legs and pats her hand.

"You're doing great. The first baby always takes the longest," the nurse says.

"How far along is she?" I ask.

"My contractions are three minutes apart," Serena cries.

"It might take a while," the nurse says. "She's still in early labor."

Serena whimpers at this news.

The nurse checks the monitor and hands my sister another cold washcloth to put on her forehead. She gives me a fresh thermos full of ice water. She tells Serena she'll be back in a half hour to check on her.

"Dylan, remember to use condoms," Serena says as the nurse closes the door. I laugh a little.

"You weren't using condoms?" I ask her.

"Not all the time."

I frown. "Mike should have known better."

She shakes her head. "It was me," she said. "Seriously, it was me. I was the stupid one."

I guess now isn't the time to lecture her about birth control.

"When I found out I was pregnant, I almost got an abortion," she says. "But I wasn't old enough, and I didn't want to tell Mom."

I wipe her wet forehead with the washcloth. "Oh, honey," I say.

"Then I knew I couldn't go through with it. I love Mike too much."

"I think you made the right decision," I say. "You're going to love this baby. So many people will love him. I already love him so much."

"I don't know what I'm doing, Dylan. I don't know how to be a mom." Her dark eyes stare helplessly into mine.

"Nobody does," I tell her. "You'll figure it out. You have Mike, you have family. Just let us help you, Serena. Don't think you have to go through this on your own. We want to be here."

She nods. Another contraction hits and I hold her hand and tell her how amazing she is and how strong she is and what a great job she's doing. She holds onto my arm.

"Dylan will you stay in LA with me? I know Mom offered, but she can be so smothering. I want you here. I need your help."

I look down at my sister and nod.

"Of course I will," I say. "I'll move here. I'll stay as long as you need me." I lean down and kiss her damp forehead. I look out the window at the ocean, at my new home, Los Angeles. It feels right. It feels perfect. I feel my anchor drop.

For the first time in my life, I realize that home isn't where you want to be. It's where you need to be.

Gray

I sit outside the delivery room with Mike. He is actually watching a birthing video on his phone. Poor bastard. I get cramming for a test at the last minute, we've all been there, but this guy takes procrastination to a new level.

There are two other delivery rooms in the corner of the hospital wing and nurses in blue scrubs speed walk back and forth between them. Every once in a while a pregnant woman in a white robe waddles out, supported by a tired, helpless, freaked out looking guy. One woman pushes an IV along with her. They all walk for a minute or two and then freeze, crouch over and scream as if they're being squeezed to death by a boa constrictor.

I cover my face in my hands. Why don't middle schools send kids to labor and delivery rooms as a class field trip? It would scare all of them into celibacy for twenty years. Why am I even here? Where are Serena's parents? Dylan called them from the road and they were trying to book a flight.

I look at Mike. "Have you talked to Serena's mom?" I ask.

Mike shakes his head. "Serena hasn't spoken to her mom in weeks."

"That doesn't mean *you* can't call her," I point out. "She should know how her daughter's doing." He sets down his phone and looks at me.

"And incur the wrath of Serena? No way. I would love to call them, but Serena made me swear I wouldn't talk to her parents. You've seen how she acts."

I nod. "She's a little feisty," I venture.

"Feisty? She's A-list nuts. She used to be so mellow. And happy. Before she was pregnant she was actually a nice person. I don't even think she swore."

"Why did you stay with her?" I ask.

He shrugs. "Her boobs grew four sizes," he says and I almost laugh.

"I'm kidding," he says. "Well, I'm not, but that's not why I stayed with her. I fell in love with her the second I saw her," he says. "It just happened. You never plan these things—and they seem to happen at the worst possible moment. Life has an amazing sense of humor."

"What happened?" I ask. "You guys just ran away together?"

"No," Mike says. "We met at one of my shows. I was in town for a few weeks visiting family in Wisconsin and that's when we started hanging out all the time. Then I had to be on the road again doing gigs and I took a comedy workshop in New York, so we couldn't see each other this summer. She started acting weird whenever we talked on the phone. I drove out and surprised her last month and found out she wasn't twenty-one, like she had said she was. She was seventeen and knocked up."

"Ouch," I say.

"Yeah. I can't even joke about that one. Statutory rape jokes get you booed off the stage pretty quick." He sighs. "But, the more I think about it, this messed up journey we've been on, the more it all makes sense. If Serena wasn't pregnant we probably wouldn't be together. And the unbelievable thing about it is, for the first time in my life, I have a plan. I'm twenty-seven years old and I'm finally figuring things out. First your life blows up in your face and then it settles in all the right places."

I nod. I can testify to that.

"So, what's up with you and Dylan?" Mike asks. "Are you two together?"

"No," I say and look out at the lobby. "We tried. Life got in the way."

Mike nods. "Serena talks about her a lot. She's crazy about Dylan. She says Dylan is one of those people that, when life hands her lemons, she makes extremely sweet lemonade."

I smirk. "That's not right," I say. "When life hands Dylan lemons, she learns how juggle," I say. "She has her own way of doing everything."

"Wow," Mike says. "I get what you're saying."

I nod. "There's no one like her," I say.

"Dude," he says. "We are being such chicks right now, dishing out our feelings," he says. "It must be all of these opened vaginas everywhere," he says. "Speaking of vaginas," he looks back at his phone and opens a new video on YouTube. I'm careful to avoid looking at the screen.

"Oh, God," Mike says and watches the phone with horror in his eyes. "Her…she just…it ripped. Argh." He covers his hand over his mouth and sprints for the bathroom. I watch him go and hope he makes it to the toilet.

A second later, Dylan runs out of the delivery room. Sweat is glistening on her forehead. She looks around the waiting area.

"Where's Mike?" she asks.

"In the bathroom throwing up," I say simply. "Apparently home birthing videos are pretty graphic. How's Serena?"

"She's dilated eight centimeters."

I don't know what she's talking about but I just nod because I don't want her to explain the gory details.

"We need Mike," Dylan says. "It's almost time to push."

"It's almost over?" I ask. I hope.

Dylan shrugs. "Serena's body doesn't want to cooperate. She's exhausted. And Luke is taking his time." Dylan rubs her hands over her eyes.

Mike staggers back to the chairs, his face pale. He wipes his mouth with the side of his hand.

"Has the beast summoned me?" he asks.

Dylan nods and waves him in.

"You should take a break, Dylan," I say. "Let Mike take over for a while."

She shakes her head. "I promised her I wouldn't leave," she says.

"Can I do anything?" I ask. "Other than video tape her birth. I'm not going back in that room." Dylan smiles and shakes her head.

"Will you just hang out?" she asks. "I like knowing you're out here," she says.

"Sure," I say. "I won't leave until everyone's fine," I promise. Dylan nods and she follows Mike through the door.

I wait and watch the clock. Time lengthens and stretches. An hour goes buy. Then two. I stare out the window across the room and I can see the ocean in the distance. Thoughts come forward and recede again in my mind like the waves and I am tossed along. I need Serena to be okay. She has to be okay. I start to feel acid in my stomach.

Dylan suddenly touches my arm and knocks me out of my trance. Her face is worried and my stomach buckles.

"She's not okay," Dylan says. "She had an epidural, but the baby can't get out of the birth canal. They're taking her in for a c-section," Dylan says.

"Will that work?" I ask. "Will she be okay?" I ask.

"I think so," she sighs. "She can't push anymore and they're worried about the baby. His heart rate is fluctuating too much. This is hard on him, too," Dylan says. She slumps down next to me.

A few minutes later, they wheel Serena down the hall toward surgery. Mike's face is as pale as porcelain. Even his lips look white. Serena's eyes are closed and her wet hair is matted to the white sheets like spilled black ink. I look away and close my eyes. It's too familiar. The past is coming back in waves and I try to shut it out. Memories threaten to resurface.

I count the seconds on the clock. I bite my knuckles. Dylan is on the phone with her mom, whose flight is delayed and she's stranded. Nothing is working out. They won't get here in time for Serena's surgery. They're too late. It's too familiar.

A half an hour later Mike comes running down the hall. He's practically skipping. The look on his face makes relief pour over me.

"We have a boy!" he says. Dylan jumps up and screams and I take a full, solid breath and run my hands over my hair.

"He's perfect. Exactly eight pounds," he says.

"And Serena?" Dylan asks.

"She's the happiest I've ever seen her. And I've seen her laugh so hard she snorts."

I stand up and Dylan jumps into my arms, hugging me so hard it almost knocks me over.

"When can I see them?" Dylan asks.

"They're washing him up," Mike says. "Serena's still in surgery. She'll be out soon."

Dylan follows Mike down the hall and they disappear behind two white folding doors. I'm so relieved I could fall over. I look around the hospital wing and don't know what to do with myself. I don't know if I'm hungry or exhausted or thirsty or all of the above. I just know I need to move.

I take the elevator down to the first floor and it's full of people coming in and out and wheelchairs and commotion. I spot the gift shop across the room.

Birth. Celebration. Gifts. Perfect.

I walk inside and this old lady with glasses halfway down her nose greets me with a smile.

I look around and try to grasp what to buy a runaway, teenage, unwed mother. I grab a handful of balloons that say congratulations. I grab some flowers—that seems fitting. There's a bakery section, with rolls and donuts and muffins and I grab a six pack of assorted muffins because this also seems appropriate. The donuts look mouth watering, so I grab a half-dozen of those, too. Then I pass some photo frames and there's a square one that's blue around the edges and in yellow loopy writing it says, "It's a boy!"

I grab that too, and pay for everything at the checkout. Five minutes later I walk down the hallway trying to balance all of my purchases. I feel strange and somewhat used and it dawns on me. My mom and sister used to talk about it and I always shrugged it off, but now I can officially say it.

I have just stress shopped.

***

When I get back upstairs the nurse informs me they've moved Serena to the recovery wing. I walk down white corridors through doors that buzz open like I'm on the Starship Enterprise. I'm wondering if I'll reach a transporter pad and get beamed to Serena's room.

I look for the room number the nurse gave me and the door is ajar so I tap it open.

"Hey," Dylan says. She's in a chair by the bed, holding Luke. Serena's sitting up in bed, her back braced by about four pillows. Mike is sitting at her other side. They all look at me and the armful of shiny colorful objects in my arms.

"Hey. Congratulations," I say. I set the vase of flowers on the counter in front of the bed. I set the balloons next to the window. I put the muffins and donuts on a table in the corner of the room.

"Wow, feeling generous?" Mike observes.

I hand him the plastic bag, completely embarrassed. He opens it and pulls out the chintzy frame I just wasted thirty five bucks on.

"Nice, something I can actually use." He holds it up for us all to admire. "A baby beer coaster!"

"It's a frame you idiot," Serena says.

Mike stands up. "Thanks man," he says and throws an arm around me like we're brothers. I almost have the urge to hug him back. I can feel the room swell with joy and love and a perfect weight of relief.

Dylan hands Luke off to Mike and Mike's eyes are mesmerized. He bends down close to Serena until their faces are inches apart.

"I love you baby."

"I love you too."

"Will you marry me?" He cradles Luke against him and gets down on one knee. I look at Dylan and her mouth is hanging open, her eyes wide with amazement.

"I'm serious, Serena. Will you please marry me?" He looks doubtful and Serena laughs. Her eyes are flooding with tears.

"Yes. Of course I'll marry you."

He leans down to her and they're kissing and cradling the baby between them and it's one of the purest things I've ever seen. I look down at my feet. We're all quiet for a few seconds and I lean my head down and whisper in Dylan's ear.

"Should I go get some more balloons?" I ask.

Dylan

I reach out and touch the sunshine gleaming on the window ledge. The heat feels like happiness and I want to grab onto it. I lean my forehead against the warm glass and look down at the Pacific Ocean, sapphire blue in the bright sun. I can see all the way down to the Santa Monica Pier.

It's my second time in Los Angeles, and she intrigues me. She is a city of many faces. She is elegant, mysterious, enchanting, dark, melancholy, and abused. She wears so many personalities. Her mood changes as quickly as her streets. Her neighborhoods are her costumes. She can never make up her mind and we have that in common. I can't wait to get to know her. I think we'll be good friends.

"Nice penthouse view for a newborn," I observe. We're alone in the delivery room. Mike and Gray left to grab something to eat.

"Too bad Luke can barely see anything yet," Serena says. I look down at his glassy eyes that squint wearily at the outdoor light flooding in. I try to memorize his face but it's like trying to take in a panoramic view. Just when one thing catches my eyes, something else distracts me. I lean down and press my nose against his smooth forehead and breathe him in. Newborn babies smell like warm rolls baking.

My sister asks for Luke by opening up her arms and I place him in her hands. I look down at him, at his little head stuffed inside a blue stocking cap, and I'm amazed how much a heart can grow and change and make room to love someone so quickly and effortlessly. A protective instinct comes over me. I just want Luke to be happy. The thought of lugging him around the country and living out of hotel rooms so Mike can perform in seedy nightclubs (with way too much black décor) makes me cringe.

"What are you guys going to do?" I ask.

"Well, believe it or not, we have an idea," Serena says.

I raise my eyebrows.

"Mike's aunt lives in Santa Monica. That's why he scheduled his tour to end out here. We're moving into her house. She's older, never married, no kids. I guess being an entertainment lawyer is pretty time consuming," Serena says. "But it pays really well," she adds. "She has a house four blocks up from the beach."

My mouth drops open. I am almost jealous of my sister.

"And LA is a great place for Mike to be. His agent lives out here. He might even get some acting jobs."

"He has an agent?" I ask, surprised.

"He's really serious about his career," she says. "He has all these plans to write and do sketch comedy and podcasts. He's the most motivated person I've ever met. He just acts like a slacker."

I can't believe it. My little sister grew up. What I saw as screwing up her life was only her striking out on her own path.

"I'm surprised Serena," I admit. "I didn't know you had it all figured out." I look out the window. I'm the one that's screwed up.

"I didn't expect to meet the love of my life when I was seventeen," Serena says.

"It's bad timing," I say.

"That's how we're different," she says. "You always talked about meeting Gray like it was the worst possible timing. But I think the timing is perfect. I get to spend my entire life with my best friend, the person who makes me happier than anyone. I get to be young with him *and* grow old with him. I didn't have to wait to meet him until I was fifty years old. It's the greatest thing that ever could have happened. But Mom and Dad, even you, wouldn't accept that. You all said I was too young." She shakes her head. "I didn't want to hear it anymore. That's why I ran away."

"Not everybody is ready to settle down when they're eighteen," I point out, but Serena shakes her head.

"It's not settling down. It's wising up. Being in a relationship doesn't tie you down. You can still go on all your crazy adventures, but it's even better, because you have a best friend to go with you."

I nod. I have to admit it. "You're right," I say.

"Are you still okay with moving in and helping me?" Serena asks. She looks hopeful.

"Of course," I say. "I promised you I would. I'm not going to back out."

"I can't pay you, but obviously you can live with us for free. Mike's aunt has three extra bedrooms."

"It's alright," I say. "I actually do pretty well with photography."

She studies me. "What about Gray?" she asks.

I shrug. I'm wondering the same thing. What about Gray? That question could be the title of my memoir.

"You don't want to follow him to Albuquerque?" she asks.

I shake my head. "I tried that once," I said. "The word 'follow' doesn't really apply to me."

She nods. "That's true. You could never be a follower," she says. She looks down at Luke for a few seconds. "You liked living in Albuquerque, right?" she asks.

I sit in the sunlight on the window ledge. "I loved it, but I always felt like I was a visitor living in Gray's world. It never felt right. I was changing too much to try and fit in, and Gray called me out on it. That's why we broke up."

"He wanted you to change?" she asks.

"No," I say. "That was the problem. He didn't want me to change. Gray's the only person I've ever met who gets me. He would never try to change me. But I felt like I was living out his dream and it was holding me back from all the things I wanted to do."

Serena pieces this all together. "Well, if you wanted to leave, if you wanted to be with Gray, I would understand. I wouldn't be mad."

"Thanks," I tell her. "But right now I need to be here with you."

She sighs with relief and smiles. Serena is so calm and happy, holding onto Luke as if her arms were molded for his curled frame.

"I'm glad it's all falling into place for you," I say.

"Finally," she says and leans her head back on the pillows.

"For the time being?" I joke and she shakes her head.

"Forever," she says and looks out the window at the shimmering skyline.

Gray

Mike and Dylan and I take turns holding Luke in the recovery room. I'm not a huge baby person, but Luke has spiky black hair and blue-gray eyes that already can focus a little. I swear I catch him smile. He's wearing a blue stocking cap that has shark eyes and a mouth. I'm jealous at how cool kids' stuff is.

Half eaten muffins and donuts litter paper plates strewn around the countertops. The television is turned onto baseball. A relaxed silence has settled around the room. Mostly, everyone is just exhausted.

I'm sitting next to Dylan in the corner of the room, behind a table, and she's showing me pictures on her camera. She documented everything: the hospital room, the scale, the chrome sink Luke was washed in, the hands of the doctor who delivered him. Luke's purple hands and feet and nose. She says she's going to make a collage, or maybe a baby book titled *The Day You Were Born*. Her gift ideas are a lot more creative than my lousy attempt. I forgot how much I missed the click of her camera, how it had become such a familiar sound, like a spot in the staircase that always creaks, or a heater tapping. They are sounds you become accustomed to because they sound like home.

Serena suddenly speaks up. "Favorite movie ending of all times," she says to all of us. "Go."

"*Karate Kid*," Mike says.

"*The Hangover*," I say. "The closing credits are the best part of the movie."

"I loved the ending of *Twilight*," Serena says, "simply because it *ended* and I didn't have to sit through the terrible movie one second longer."

"*Sixteen Candles*," Dylan says. I look over at her.

"It doesn't star Tom Hanks and Meg Ryan," I say with surprise.

"Long Duck Dong is the greatest character name of all times," Mike says. "I'll give you that."

"Every girl goes to mush at the end of *Sixteen Candles*," Dylan claims and Serena nods in agreement.

"Why?" Mike and I ask at the same time.

"It's every girls dream," Serena says. "Hot, popular guy falls for nerdy awkward girl. And he picks her up in a Porsche? You can't beat that."

"That's it?" Mike asks. "The guy drives a nice car, and it's the greatest ending of all time? You two will fit in so well in Los Angeles."

"No," Dylan says, her face thoughtful. "It's the feeling at the end of the movie that gets me. It's like a fantasy. I can't describe why it's so good. You just have to see it."

I lean my head to the side and think about this.

Suddenly the door swings open and a dozen colorful balloons come sailing into the room in front of two frantic, frazzled looking adults.

"Serena!" Dylan's mom exclaims. I've never met Dylan's parents, but I can tell immediately that it's her. She has the same freckly face and narrow nose. Her hair is strawberry blond, lighter than Dylan's, and her eyes are greener but she has the same smile and pale pink lips.

I look over at her dad, and I remember Dylan telling me he isn't her biological father. Her real dad has been out of her life since she was young. I watch him set down the balloons, and a card, and a box, and a gift bag. Apparently he is also the victim of stress shopping.

Serena sits up in bed, a little stiffly, and her mom bends down to hug her. She wipes hair off of Serena's forehead to kiss her and then she's immediately clawing the air for Luke. Dylan scoots her chair back and stands up and offers her parents a hug.

I stay in my seat in the corner of the room and watch the family reunion unfold.

Mike takes a hesitant step toward Dylan's dad and extends his hand.

"Good to see you again, Dean," Mike says carefully. I watch their interaction and wonder if Dean would rather punch Mike in the face. He slowly extends his hand and shakes Mike's, but he doesn't smile. Dean's tall and he's balding. He spikes the dark hair he has left so he looks like some kind of a CEO for a record label.

"Is it true?" Dylan's mom asks. Her eyes pass between Mike and Serena. "Are you two engaged?"

From the anxious look on her face, I can't tell if Dylan's mom wants the rumor to be validated.

Mike nods. "I asked her a couple of hours ago," he said. "It seemed an appropriate time, when she was still doped up on drugs and didn't have the sense to say no."

No one objects to this reasoning.

"She doesn't have a ring yet." He looks over at Serena. "I figure you might want to help pick it out?"

Serena nods. "I don't trust your taste in jewelry. If it were up to you, it would be a pink diamond in the shape of a heart."

Mike shakes his head. "You know I can do better than that. I was thinking more a *Lord of the Rings* design. We could each get gold bands with an inscription along the side that stands out when it's heated. I've already been thinking about the words. *One ring to find us, one ring to bind us and in marriage to forever unite us.*"

I try not to laugh.

"Wouldn't that be romantic?" Mike asks.

"No," Serena and her mother say at the same time.

"When will the wedding be?" her mom asks.

"Soon," Serena says. "Before you guys head back home, once I'm out of the hospital. Mike's aunt has a friend who can officiate it," Serena says. "We just want something small, on the beach."

Dylan's parents look at each other and nod. They know better than to say no.

"I need to make this legal before she changes her mind," Mike says.

I look at Dylan and all the hostility in her eyes has vanished. She's actually smiling at him.

"Well, you two make cute babies, I can say that much," Dylan's mom says and presses her lips to Luke's forehead.

I stand up from the corner seat to offer my chair and Dylan's mom looks over at me. She studies me for a few seconds.

"Are you a friend of Mike's?" she asks.

"He's like a brother to me," Mike nods, and I roll my eyes.

"Wait," Dylan's mom says. She blinks hard and squints her eyes at me. "I swear, you look just like Gray," she says. "Dylan, doesn't he look a lot like that baseball player you showed me pictures of? The one you met in Phoenix, who you always called The Love of Your Life? Or your Soulmate? Or your Future Husband?"

Everyone turns to stare at me. If this were a movie with subtitles, the caption 'awkward silence' would work nicely right now.

"That is Gray, Mom," Dylan says. "Gray, this my mom, Gail. And my dad, Dean."

Her mom hands the baby off to Mike and walks towards me. I reach my hand out to shake hers, but she stretches out both of her arms and I know she won't settle for less than hug. I have to duck to meet her. Dylan's dad must have been tall.

She leans back and looks in my eyes. "I'm so happy to finally meet you," she says. "If I hadn't talked to you on the phone that one time, I would have sworn you were just one of Dylan's made-up travel stories."

Sometime I feel like I am.

She looks across the room at Dylan. "I thought you were driving with Nick?" she asks. She lets go of my waist, but one of her hands holds onto my arm, as if she's afraid I'm going to run off.

Dylan shakes her head, sadly. "Orson died in Omaha."

"Who the hell is Orson?" Mike asks.

"Where the hell is Omaha?" Serena asks.

"Nebraska," I clarify.

"Hey, what do you call a really hot girl in Nebraska?" Mike asks and we all turn to look at him.

"A tourist," he says.

I start to crack up and Serena shakes her head at me. "Don't encourage his bad jokes," she says.

Dylan's mom looks between me and Mike. "You boys are going to fit in very well in this family."

"Nebraska is a lovely state, full of lovely people," Dylan says, defensively.

"Who do you know in Nebraska?" Serena demands.

"Chris and Sue Anne," Dylan informs her family. "We practically owe them our lives. A tornado almost lifted our car off the ground."

"Orson?" Her mom asks. "That thing is a barge. Nothing can lift it."

"No we were in Gray's car," Dylan clarifies.

"Just put it in a scrapbook, Dylan," Serena says.

"We also got arrested," she adds, "a few nights ago in Texas. I picked up a wanted felon and offered him a ride."

Everyone laughs out loud at this and I look around with surprise. No one believes her. Dylan meets my eyes and she shrugs like she's used to it. She told me once that I'm the only person who understands her, who asks to see her pictures and listens to her stories. I didn't believe it when she told me; I figured everyone appreciated her like I do. But she was telling me the truth. Dylan doesn't need to exaggerate or embellish. She lives all her crazy thoughts out loud.

Her mom's eyes brighten. "Well, I'm so happy you two got back together." She looks between Dylan and me and waits for one of us to confirm her statement. We're both silent. I'm waiting for Dylan to talk first.

"You are back together?" her mom asks. I can feel everyone looking at me.

"We drove here together," I offer. Dylan looks down at the ground.

A confused crease appears in the middle of her mom's forehead. I start to smile. Dylan's actions are probably the direct cause of that wrinkle line.

"Wait a second," her mom says. "Orson died on the highway, and Gray just happened to be there, in Omaha, to offer you a ride?"

"Technically his girlfriend offered me a ride," Dylan says.

"My fictional girlfriend," I clarify.

"What?" her mom asks.

"It's a long story," Dylan finishes.

"It always is with you," her dad says.

I'm afraid to look at Dylan. I look at the balloons instead. There's no way to explain our situation. I feel like we're breaking up again, but when did we ever get back together?

"I'm really confused," Serena says.

I stare at her. *You're* confused?

"Are you two waiting for an even bigger sign that you're meant to be together?" Serena asks. "Do you need a meteor to drop out of the sky saying GET MARRIED on it and land at your feet?"

Probably.

"Our relationship usually falls under the heading of Crappy Timing,'" I explain.

The room is quiet. Even Luke appears to be interested in the outcome of our conversation. Dylan's mom sighs and she gives up on the topic.

"Well, Gram and Pop are at the hotel," she says.

"You brought Grandma and Grandpa out here?" Serena moans.

"We had to. It's their first great grandchild. Your aunt's on her way too, with your cousins. They'll get in tonight."

"This is exactly why I ran away," Serena states. "Does everything have to be a family event?"

"Yes," Dylan and her mom say at the same time. I can see why Dylan left after high school. She needed to stretch out, and she couldn't do that at home. Serena starts talking wedding plans with Dylan and her mom.

Dylan's dad walks over to me and extends his hand. "I'm Dean," he says. "Nice to finally meet you."

I nod and shake his hand.

"I've been reading *Baseball Weekly* this summer, keeping tabs on you. Your name was all over the place. I heard the Dodgers are interested?"

I nod. "My agent's going back and forth with them," I say. "I'm not sure if I want to sign or play another year at school. Their offer would have to be pretty good."

The baby suddenly interrupts us with a hungry wail. Everyone in the room sucks in a breath and lets it out with an "awww," and it's amazing what you find yourself able to love.

I excuse myself so Serena can nurse and her family can talk wedding details. An edge of jealousy sets in and I don't want to hear about their happily ever after, how all their mistakes turned into a victory. Most of my victories turn out to be mistakes. Thanks a lot, Fate.

I walk slowly to the elevator. I'm still wondering why I ran into Dylan in Omaha. Serena's right. Do we need an even bigger sign that we're meant to be together?

I have about a week of sleep to catch up on and my feet drag down the hallway. I could use a nap before I hit the road. I head down to the lobby and I'm greeted by the noise of footsteps and voices and overhead announcements. I look around at all the people sitting and waiting, like we're in a strange airport going nowhere.

I sit in the lobby and watch people coming and going. I watch people walking in with balloons and flowers, with smiles and excitement. Other people walk in looking anxious and forlorn. It is the most emotionally charged place on earth.

I close my eyes and lean back in the seat. The last time I was in a hospital was the night of my sister's death. I haven't stepped inside one since. Walking in the emergency room doors was like pushing my way through a brick wall. I was afraid I was going to walk right into Amanda's ghost.

My brain is a myriad of thoughts that refuse to have ending points, just jumbles and knots and loose strings. I need answers.

I keep replaying Mike's proposal to Serena. How perfect it all was. How she was nodding before he even finished asking. How much I would give for Dylan to react that way to me.

I sigh and open my eyes. They're so dry they burn. I want to leave and drive around or walk or run until my knees give out. I grab my cell phone out of my pocket and there's a text from Lenny. A text. Wow. She must really be worried about me. I read the message.

I'm worried about you. Did you work things out with Dylan?

I call her number and after a few rings, Lenny picks up.

"Hey. Are you okay?"

The concern in her voice makes my throat knot. I swallow because I can't lie to Lenny.

"I'm messed up," I say and run a hand over my head. My thoughts feel heavy, like rocks. Is love just an illusion, a mean trick that life plays on you? It diffracts your world into brilliant colors but is it ever constant? Is there a way to make it permanent?

"I don't care about baseball," I hear myself say.

"Gray, don't be stupid. You're amazing at baseball. Didn't you get some VIP trophy this summer?"

I roll my eyes. "MVP, not VIP." Why is that so hard to remember?

"Sorry. I don't speak meathead."

"Thanks."

"Gray, you need to stick with baseball. You love it. And you could make a ton of cash, are you nuts?"

"It's just a game," I say. "It's just entertainment. Maybe I should just be with Dylan. I always expected her to follow me. Follow my life, my dreams, my path. And I was pissed off when she didn't want to, when it didn't fall perfectly into place the way I wanted it. So instead of trying to work it out, I pushed her away. That was the biggest mistake of my life."

"What are you saying?"

I bite my lips together. What am I saying?

"Maybe I should give something up. I might be okay with that. I can do something else. I can finish school. Maybe I could coach."

I breathe out a sigh.

Lenny breathes out a sigh. It's like an echo.

"I wouldn't even be playing baseball right now if it wasn't for Dylan," I add. I'm grabbing for excuses. "I'd probably still be in Phoenix, living with my parents, hating my life."

"That's not true," Lenny says. "Dylan helped you get back on your feet, but you did the rest on your own. You're just delusional right now. You're suffering from a post sex high. Your hormones are all out of whack. You can't make any rational decisions."

"Yeah, right," I laugh.

"I'm serious. You have sex brain. It's basically making you stupid. When sex is on the brain you have no common sense, logic or practicality. It's dangerous, Gray. Let it wear off for at least two days before you make any life-altering decisions."

I smile. She might be right.

"Is Bubba there?" I ask. "Is he telling you to say this?"

"We broke up," she says. "Last month."

She doesn't sound sad about it, more like she's stating a fact. I almost say I'm sorry, but sometimes breaking up is the best thing you can do. I never felt like Bubba was good enough for her.

"Congratulations," I say, instead.

"Thank you," she says. "I told you I don't date athletes."

"You can do better," I say.

"Yeah. I never believed in the whole stupid soul mate thing. What a load of bullshit. But, when I saw you and Dylan together, I started to believe in it. I want to hold out for something like that. Is that a cheesy thing to say?"

"No," I say, because she's right.

I say goodbye to Lenny and slip the phone in my pocket.

I stretch out over a row of chairs and stare up at the ceiling tiles, speckled in flecks of gray and black. I wish Amanda were here. I still need her sometimes. I breathe out her name. Amanda, what do I do now? Can you help me out here? Give me a sign?

I close my eyes and there is something strangely comforting about all the commotion around me. I fade off to sleep.

Dylan

The sun is starting to set and I know Gray wants to get on the road. He isn't answering his phone and I can't find him anywhere. Finally, on the first floor by the gift shop, I see him asleep on a row of chairs. I sit down on the edge of one of the seats and lean my back against his hip. I rest my hand on his shoulder. I feel him shift and wake up.

"People are heading out," I say.

He moans in response and swings his arm over his face to block out the bright overhead fluorescent lights.

"Do you want to go back to the hotel and sleep?" I offer. "Or you can stay at Mike's aunt's house?"

I know there's an edge to my voice, a plea, because I don't want him to leave yet. My family never understands me and he does and I want him here. I'm not ready to say goodbye. I will never be ready to say goodbye.

Gray sits up and rubs his eyes. "I need to get home," he says. "I have to be back at school in a week, and I promised my parents I'd hang out for a few days."

I nod slowly.

"You took a pretty long detour," I say.

"It's been interesting. Mike's a good guy, Dylan. He's going to be really good for your sister."

"Can we take a walk before you leave?" I ask and Gray nods and grabs my hand. We stand up and walk through the automatic doors and we're welcomed with fresh air. We turn and head toward the beach.

Gray's phone rings and he looks down at the screen and hesitates. He tells me he needs to take it. "It's my agent," he says. "The greediest man I've ever met."

He stops at the corner and sits down on the sidewalk bench and I keep walking down the block to give him space. I listen to the sounds of the city, to the traffic, the tires, the impatient brake and acceleration of cars like a conversation that suddenly cuts off and continues again. I watch people on the sidewalk in front of me and see a hurried frenzy, a nervous gesture, an awkward tick. But then I look at the ocean and I relax. If I'm going to live in LA, I need to be close to the ocean. It keeps you humble. She's like a big sister, offering advice, reminding me to slow down and focus on what's important.

Gray catches up with me a couple minutes later, just as our shoes hit the sand. My hair blows into my eyes and I pull it back into a short stump of a ponytail. We kick off our shoes and sit down, facing the setting sun, an orange apricot hanging low in the sky.

I look over at Gray. "You have a crease right here," I tell him. I point my finger between his eyebrows. "It's your 'I have serious thoughts in my head,' crease."

He smiles because it's true.

"What's your plan, Dylan?" he asks me.

I look back out at the water and suddenly the sunset is no longer beautiful. The water looks cold. It looks like a cinematic backdrop to accompany a sad ending.

"I'm going to stay in the hospital with Serena for the next few nights. She doesn't want to be alone and she said she's already getting sick of Mike's lactation references. He claims he wants to bottle breast milk and sell it as a coffee creamer. You can imagine the advertising tag lines he's coming up with."

Gray's quiet for a few seconds. He's not in a joking mood. The waves are small in the light wind, barely a ripple. They have lost their edge, or maybe they're just exhausted from their long journey.

"That doesn't answer my question," Gray says. He turns my shoulders so we're facing each other. "What's your plan, Dylan?" he repeats.

I want to say that I'm going with him to Phoenix, and back to Albuquerque and everywhere else life takes him. But that's his path and, as usual, it splits away from mine.

"I'm moving here," I say. "My sister asked me to stay and help her with Luke and I promised I would. It's where I need to be right now."

I'm expecting his eyes to fall, but he looks surprised. "You want to live in LA?" Gray asks me and I nod without hesitating.

"Ever since she asked me, it felt right. Usually when I commit to a place, I get this awful sinking feeling. I actually feel depressed. But this time it didn't happen. I want to be here." I look hopefully at Gray. "It's sort of close to New Mexico," I hint.

Gray shakes his head. "I'm not living in New Mexico anymore," he says.

This time I feel a crease in my forehead. "But you said you're going back there?"

He nods. "I have to meet with some coaches and move my stuff out, but then I'm moving here."

I look at the ocean and back at him. "To LA?" I ask. Is he joking? "I thought you were playing baseball?"

Gray smiles. "We just got the offer we wanted from the Dodgers," he says. "We're accepting it. I'm signing."

I nod slowly. The name sounds familiar, and I try to envision the mascot. What is a dodger? A type of badger? A cousin of a beaver?

"The San Francisco Dodgers?" I guess and the sky immediately lightens with the idea that we could make this work. "We would be in the same state?"

Gray rolls his eyes. "I don't care what you say, I'm officially giving you an intro to baseball class," he says. "The Los Angeles Dodgers," he clarifies. "The stadium's right downtown."

"Wait," I say. "We're both moving to LA?"

He hesitates to answer me as if he'll jinx this entire moment. He nods once. "Yes?"

Goosebumps rise up on my arms. Gray leans forward and rests his forehead against mine. I lace my fingers through his, first his right hand and then his left. It sends a jolt of energy all the way through my arms, to my chest, and I wonder if our fingertips are really just extensions of our hearts. Our fingers are where every connection begins and ends. I'm afraid to speak, afraid to blink, as if this all might disappear. I hold on tight to Gray's hands.

"I don't want to be away from you. Ever," he tells me. He leans back and his eyes are inches away from mine. "I'm not letting you go this time, Dylan. You are my most basic need."

"Gray—"

"Listen, I have a theory. Want to hear it?"

I nod. I love his theories.

"Life is really simple. We're just thrown so many distractions that we forget how simple it is. But people have the most basic needs," he says. "And deep down, I think we all get it. We know what's most important. We know what we're searching for."

I nod.

"The challenge is, if you're lucky enough to make an amazing discovery, you need to be smart enough to hold onto it. If you let it fall through your fingers, it makes the whole search a waste." He looks at me, really looks at me. "I'm not letting you fall through my fingers again," he says.

It's so simple. "That is your best theory, yet," I say.

~ Two Weeks Later ~

Dylan

"What? Is? That?" I ask and stare at a sparkly pink garment draped over my sister's arm. She hands it to me and I examine the tight, glittery fabric.

"Your bridesmaid dress," Serena says.

My mom glances up from the couch, where she's reading a magazine. My Grandma is sitting next to her, knitting a sweater for Luke. My dad and Pop are watching golf on the TV. My aunt and cousins are sitting on the floor, making flower wrist corsages. My aunt Diane-Dan and her partner are here; they're in the kitchen in charge of making the wedding cake.

My mom gives me a sympathetic look. "It's not very you," she offers.

"Where did you get it?" I ask. "A store specializing in stripper costumes?" I joke. "On the sales rack?" Our fashion tastes have never exactly converged. Serena grew up in tutus and high heels, and I grew up barefoot and in overalls.

"Sorry, Dylan," she mocks. "I couldn't find any dresses made out of recycled jeans and patches."

"How do you know it will fit me?" I ask. It's my only exit door out of dress hell.

"It has a lot of spandex in it," she tells me and pulls on the stretchy fabric to demonstrate. I start to back away, but she comes at me, her eyes stubborn. "Don't you dare say no to me, Dylan. I'm very hormonal right now. I wish I could wear this but my current porn sized boobs would rip it apart."

I look down at her giant chest, covered in a white terrycloth robe. Her dark hair is pulled off her face in hot rollers, held together by what looks like giant paperclips.

"I have a black dress," I offer. I bought it four years ago and it still fits. It's the only dress I own. "Can't I just wear that?"

"You want to wear black to my *wedding*?" she says.

"Well, it's not like you're a virgin bride," I say and point to Luke, sleeping like an angel in a bassinette in the living room.

Mike walks out of the kitchen with a beer in his hand. Serena allowed him creative liberty over the frosting design on the cake, which was a dangerous choice.

"Did somebody say porn?" he asks. "Hey, I've decided on a theme for the cake. I'm going with an outer space motif," he says and Serena drops her argument with me long enough to stare at him.

"I'm thinking of the words, 'May the Force of Marriage be With You,' and I envision two lightsabers crisscrossing in the center and joining in an epic explosion of the Death Star which will be shaped like a heart."

"That's really creative," I tell him.

"Mike," Serena groans, "I said absolutely no Star Wars references."

"Can I still do outer space? Maybe have all the planets aligned and then we're joined together by the force of the cosmos?"

"Just draw me up a design first," Serena says. She turns back to me and I stare into the mass of pink sequins on the dress.

"I think can see myself reflected in it," I say.

She ignores my observation.

"It's a size six," she says, "the same size you wore to our cousin's wedding last summer. Besides, you never gain weight. Brat."

"I love you Serena, but I am not putting that on." I cross my arms over my chest. "I would rather wear duct tape from head to foot. Well, as long as there's a butt flap."

"Just try it on. If it doesn't fit, you don't have to wear it. I promise." She hands me the dress. "Never say no to a bride on her wedding day," she states, as if it's a law enforced in the state of California.

I relent and go into the bathroom. I pull on the bright, scratchy material. It actually isn't that tight. I turn in front of the full length mirror. It fits perfectly. Damn.

Serena walks in and nods with satisfaction. She confirms what I already fear.

"It fits."

"It's pink," I say.

"Its crimson rose. A very dark shade of pink. It's gorgeous."

I turn around in front of the mirror. At least it isn't too short. It falls to my knees so I look like a high-end call girl, versus you're everyday street hooker. I'm okay with it, until I walk out of the bathroom and see the shoes Serena picked out.

"Stilts?" I say.

"They're high heels," she says.

"They look like stilts. How am I going to wear these on the beach?"

"They elongate your legs, Dylan. It's flattering."

She throws them at me and I put them on. They're pink, too.

She directs me back into the bathroom. I look at myself in the mirror.

"Now, as for this hair of yours," she says and picks up a handful of my hair with a frown. "Dylan, what delinquent hair hater cut this?"

"Me," I say.

"Oh. Well, we'll just put some curls in it. At least you won't see how uneven it is." She plugs in the curling iron and shakes a bottle of hair spray. She sets down combs and picks and brushes on the countertop like she's a doctor assembling tools for surgery.

Once she's satisfied with my loose curls, she comes at me with a pencil in her hand.

"Hold still."

"Wait. Whoa. What is that?" I lean away from her outstretched arm.

"It's blue eyeliner. Just like the color I'm wearing."

I stare at the tip of the pencil like it's a burning fire poker and shake my head.

"Look, I agreed to wearing a full-length glitter tube top that astronauts can probably see from outer space, and I smell like a can of hairspray. I think I've been more than accommodating. Can you please leave my face alone?"

My sister refuses to budge. She informs me there's even more makeup to come. I look at the sparkling blue eyeliner that highlights her eyes. It looks like puffy glue and I'm afraid it will never come off. I back up toward the door.

"Mom!" I yell for help. Serena's face drops into a pout and I immediately feel guilty. "Please, Dylan?" she asks. "For me? It's my wedding day."

I sigh and sit down on the stool next to the bathroom counter. I close my eyes and hold my breath as the pencil scratches across my eyelid. Serena keeps telling me to relax my face and to breathe. This is worse than the dentist.

A half hour later, the makeover is done.

"You're beautiful," Serena says. "You're welcome."

I mumble a thank you and slip off the stool. I turn and look at my reflection before I open the door. I'm actually surprised. Serena went light on the makeup, just touching up my skin to make it all one tone. She used a light dusting of blush on my cheekbones, and my lipstick is pink, but it's a light pink that compliments my coloring. Even the blue eyeliner isn't very noticeable. It's blended into gray eye shadow.

"Now get out," Serena says. "No way are you going to look hotter than me today."

***

Six hours later my baby sister is legally married and has a child, but she's too young to drink a glass of champagne to celebrate. Laws make no sense. We walk back to the beach house and Mike's aunt has a catered steak dinner set up in their backyard. White lights are strewn around flower pots and eucalyptus trees. Two long picnic tables are covered in white linen and sprinkled with pink rose petals. I set down my phone and camera on the back steps and take off my stilts. I stretch my feet and slip on a pair of black sandals.

I walk out into the garden and grab a thin, soft eucalyptus leaf. I pull it apart and breathe in its sweet scent. My head is heavy with thoughts, all about Gray. There's been a nagging question in the back of my mind all day that I need to ask him.

Just as I turn to walk inside, I hear my cell phone ring. I pick it up off the steps and look down at the screen and I simultaneously want to laugh and cry. I missed him so much today.

"Hey," Gray's voice comes through the speaker, through my ear and punches against my heart. "How was the wedding?"

"Gorgeous," I say. "It was perfect weather, right on the beach, officiated by Mike's friend who has a voice that sounds exactly like Russell Crowe's. It's like the ocean itself was speaking."

"What are you guys doing now?" he asks. "Do you have dinner plans?"

I look around at the empty backyard. "My sister's sleeping. Everybody else is watching football. A newborn baby cuts into evening social plans."

"So, you're free?" he asks.

"I'm always free," I say.

"Excellent," he says. "There's a surprise for you outside."

I open the patio door and walk down the hallway, passing the dining room and the living room. I open the stained glass front door and look around the steps for a package or flowers. The wooden steps are empty.

"I'm not seeing anything," I say.

He laughs into the phone. There's a strange echo to his voice.

"Look around," he says.

My stomach jumps. I realize what the surprise is. I look up and down the curb, lined with parked cars. I don't see his hatchback anywhere. "Where are you?"

"I'm standing in front of my car," he says.

"I don't see your car."

"Dylan, look across the street."

I hear laughing and it sounds like it's coming from straight in front of me. I look across the street, and there he is, leaning against a black convertible. He's wearing dark, faded jeans and a red, Bob Dylan concert t-shirt. The sky is turning dark, but there's still a ribbon of neon light in the western sky.

I still have my phone to my ear. I press the receiver to my heart to see if he can hear how fast it's beating and he laughs. He puts his phone in his pocket.

He raises his hand and waves.

I clear my throat and slip into character, mustering up my best Molly Ringwald imitation. I glance up and down the sidewalk with disbelief and then I point to my chest.

"Me?" I mouth. Gray shakes his head.

"You're supposed to say, 'Yeah, you,'" I shout across the street.

"Uh-uh," he says. "This is as far as I go."

I walk across the street to meet him. "You watched the movie," I say and he nods. "Did you like the ending?" I ask.

"I understand why you like it, but it's not why you think," he tells me.

"Oh, really?" I look in his eyes, and they're lighter and happier than I've ever seen them.

"It's not the scene you remember. It's that song. That song makes the ending. A classic eighties melodramatic balled by the Thompson Twins? Possibly the sappiest crap of all time."

"By sappy you mean incredibly moving and laced with deep messages about life?"

"Sure," he says. I look past him at the black convertible.

"Sorry it's not a red Porsche," Gray says. "That's a little out of my price range."

"This is yours?" I ask him and he nods.

"My dad helped me pick it out. Signing bonuses pay pretty well," he admits. "I've never seen my dad more excited. We drove it around all week."

I run my hand over the sleek roof, cool against my skin.

"Wow," I say. "I'm naming him Black Panther."

Gray steps back so he can take in my outfit.

"You look—"

"Like a sparkly baton, I know. Not by choice, by force."

"Sorry I didn't wear my pimp suit so we could match," Gray says and I roll my eyes.

"You can blame Serena," I say. "She practically had to tie me down to give me a makeover."

"Blame her? You mean thank her profusely."

"You like my new hooker style?" I ask.

"I would never label you as that," Gray says. "I was thinking stripper," he says.

I laugh and Gray turns me around with his hand. "Perfect," he says. "It has a slit. Slits are just a starting point for ripping something off."

"Go right ahead," I say. "Right now, please."

"Oh, I will," he says and his eyes look serious. It sends an erotic jolt up my legs. "But not yet," he says.

"First we're having cake?" I ask.

"No," Gray says. "No more *Sixteen Candles*. I have a much better idea." He opens the car door for me. "Come on," he says. "We're going for a drive. I want you to see the city lights."

I slide inside and he closes the door. The smooth black leather seat brushes against my legs. I fasten the seatbelt and Gray gets in next to me.

"You need to see the sky scrapers in a convertible at night. It's the best way to see a skyline." He starts the car and shifts into gear. The engine purrs as he drives onto the road. He turns up the stereo and plays Counting Crows, album one, track eleven. I smile. It's one of my favorite songs.

I watch the houses and apartments pass until we're on Pacific Drive and suddenly the ocean is right next to us spilling onto the sand. I can smell the salty air as the wind whips against my hand. I reach my arm out—

there's no window frame to block it, no roof to enclose it. I feel like I could lasso the purple clouds in the darkening sky and reel them in. The car accelerates and we're coasting up a freeway ramp. I lean my head back against the seat rest and let the sky and the music pour over me.

"Ryan Adams is performing tonight," he tells me over the music.

Gray and I have listened to every single one of his records together. We've analyzed every song. We've had sex to every song.

"In LA?" I ask and Gray nods.

"He's playing at the Walt Disney Concert Hall," he says. "It's an amazing venue. But there aren't any tickets left." He looks over at me. "I checked. It's been sold out for weeks."

I refuse to be discouraged. Words like "sold old" only imply a challenge. You can't make an amazing discovery and let it slip through your fingers.

"Gray, this concert is a basic need. We have to try," I say.

He nods. "I thought you'd say that. If anyone can talk their way in, it's you."

He maneuvers around traffic and we fly down the freeway, surrounded by a red stream of lights in front of us, and white lights, like comets, behind us. We are in a galaxy. The downtown skyline rises in the distance like a space station. The Staples Center is lit up with purple neon lights like a futuristic landing strip.

We exit the freeway and turn down Broadway, heading for the glowing buildings. Gray was right. Everyone needs to see city lights in a convertible. I lean back, mesmerized as they approach. The skyscrapers loom around us and above us, towers of light that stretch all the way to the stars.

Gray

I slow down and point out the Walt Disney Concert Hall, a theater in the downtown music district. I love the architecture of the theater, the way it waves as if it's moving like a flag, batting in the wind. At night it's even more dramatic. A band of lights cut through the center like an electric sail. The curving steel makes it half anchor, half sail, half boat, half building.

Dylan looks out at the empty sidewalks with disappointment. A few people are scurrying up the steps to the entrance.

"I don't see anyone selling tickets," I say.

"Then we'll sneak in," Dylan informs me and I smile at her tenacity. She points at the theater. "Ryan Adams is inside that building. The only thing standing in our way is a flimsy door."

"And a lot of security," I point out.

I'm interested to see how she plans to pull this off. I turn into the underground parking garage and hand the attendant the astronomical twenty-dollar parking fee. Welcome to LA.

As soon as I find a parking spot Dylan throws the door open. I get out and run after her and we both sprint for the escalators.

"Here's the plan," she says once we reach the metal stairs. "We're local radio station journalists but we forgot our press passes."

I nod. I'm smiling at her determination. I look closely at her eyes.

"Are you wearing blue eyeliner?" I ask.

"Yes. Gray, please focus. We're publicity."

"Right," I say. "Which Los Angeles radio station do we work for?" I test her.

"Z...1...0...crap." She shakes her head. "Okay, scratch that. We need to go with something familiar. We're photographers."

"Um, no cameras?" I point out.

She slaps her hand over her forehead. I'm starting to feel bad. There's no way we're going to sneak into this venue. I'm just getting Dylan's hopes up.

"The one time I don't have my camera," she says.

The escalator reaches the ground floor, and we're inside the theater lobby. Dylan scopes out each usher standing guard as if she's testing for weaknesses. There's a dwindling crowd inside. People stand next to the bar, slamming the last sip of their overpriced drinks. A mix of cologne and perfume fragrances drifts through the air. The overhead lights flash, a sign that the show is about to start.

"Please take your seats," the ushers shout as if they're teasing us.

"We should split up," she whispers to me. "You take the female ushers, and I'll take the males. If Plan A doesn't work, we'll reconvene in five minutes and figure out Plan B."

"What's Plan B?" I ask. "Abort mission?"

"Never. We'll break in," Dylan says.

"Good luck with that," I say after her as she approaches an usher standing between two red velvet ropes. I make my way to the front entrance.

I walk outside and turn in a circle, taking in the steel walls of the theater that curve and sweep the sky.

I head towards the Will Call, next to the box office. I give the girl behind the partition my credit card and she looks up my name and hands me the two tickets I bought last week when I heard the show was in town. She smiles at me as she slides the tickets under the glass window.

"Enjoy the show," she says. I grab the tickets just as Dylan is walking out the front doors. Her face looks wounded by rejection. Her eyes trail the architecture of the theater, all the way to the roof as if she's planning to scale the walls.

I hold the tickets in my hand and walk up to her. "What happened with the usher?" I ask.

She shrugs. "He didn't believe I was Ryan Adams' personal trainer."

"He's a rock star," I point out. "Maybe you should have gone with personal drug dealer?"

"I must be losing my touch," Dylan says. She looks around at the empty terrace. "At least we tried."

"Well, then I'm glad I bought some tickets," I say and hand her one. She stares down at the white ticket. RYAN ADAMS is printed in bold black letters, above the word ADMSSION. She looks at me.

"Surprise," I say.

"You had these all along?"

"I picked them up at Will Call. I ordered them last week, which was a good thing, since it did sell out."

She stares at the ticket in her hand like she's holding a sheet of gold.

"Wow," she says. She traces her finger over the ticket. "This is the greatest surprise of my life." She looks up at me. "Gray, do you still want to marry me?"

I look down at her and my voice is suddenly stuck in my throat. Her eyes are serious.

"Will you ask me again?" she says.

"To marry you?"

She nods. "Not right now. But someday, will you ask me again?"

All I can do is smile. I feel my entire body, my complete wholeness, from my head to my feet, to the goosebumps raised out on my skin. I realize Dylan's never been my sad song. She's my favorite song. The one I want to play over and over again.

"Promise?" she asks. The wind tosses her wavy hair over her eyes and I brush it away. Her eyes are the most sincere I've ever seen. I take a deep breath and it feels like I'm inhaling the sky, the stars, and all the lights around me.

"Promise you'll say yes?" I ask.

"Yes," Dylan says without hesitating.

"I promise," I say.

She sticks her thumb out to grab mine and I wrap my thumb around hers and seal it. I let go and reach for her face and rake my fingers through her hair, pulling her lips towards mine. I close my eyes and lean down and kiss her.

I know I still have a lot to figure out. My future isn't set, but I consider that a good thing. It keeps it open to possibilities. Right now all I know is this: I have all that I need with me, all that I want, in my hands. No matter where my life goes, it won't be boring. It won't be perfect. But I found love and I'm holding onto it. Finally, forever.

THE END

Finally, Forever **Playlist:**

1. Omaha – Counting Crows
2. Your Wildest Dreams – The Moody Blues
3. Iko Iko – The Belle Stars
4. Cameras – Matt and Kim
5. Two Atoms in a Molecule – Noah and the Whale
6. Everlasting Arms – Vampire Weekend
7. Call it Off – Tegan and Sara
8. Samsonite Man – Fashawn
9. Faith – George Michael
10. The End of That – Plants and Animals
11. 2,000 Miles – KT Tunstall
12. Ho Hey – The Lumineers
13. Unless It's Kicks – Okkervil River
14. Your Love – The Outfield
15. Bye Bye Bye – Plants and Animals
16. Hospital – Counting Crows
17. La Cienega Just Smiled –Ryan Adams
18. A Murder of One – Counting Crows
19. My Favorite Song – KaiserCartel
    **The last song on this playlist, and what I consider to be Gray and Dylan's theme song for the entire series is:
20. Everlasting Love – U2

Finally, Forever **deleted scene:**
(In the story, this scene would have appeared near the end of the book, a week before Serena and Mike's wedding—before Gray surprises Dylan in Los Angeles.)

Gray

My dad and I walk into The Coffee Bean and Tea Leaf in Scottsdale, Arizona. It's ninety-five degrees outside, and it isn't even 10 am yet. My dad walks to the counter to order iced coffees before we drive out to an Audi dealership to look at some new cars in the showroom.

My agent called me yesterday and announced my signing bonus. It's higher than most people's yearly salaries. My dad insisted I invest in a new car, and I really can't argue with him. My hatchback has seen enough years and miles to be considered suitable for Dylan. I plan on giving it to her. Besides, you can't live in LA without a car—it's like not having legs.

We walk inside the coffee shop and I'm amazed at all the tan, toned, beautiful people. For a second I feel like I'm standing in line for an audition. Scottsdale is the ritzy burrow of Phoenix—it's like living inside a television sitcom where everyone could be a runway model. Girls in halter tops and short skirts and high heels stand in line to order, looking at cell phones or typing on cell phones or talking on cell phones. A few of them glance over at me and smile, these flirty smiles highlighted with white teeth. I smile back and a feeling of relief comes over me because I can officially say I'm not single. I don't have to strike up a conversation with these girls, I don't have to wonder about them or build up expectations and be disappointed. Some people are great at being single, they thrive, but I always preferred being in a relationship. Maybe it's because I grew up with a twin—I was used to having this other half at my side all the time. I was used to someone constantly aware and assessable and that became my idea of normal.

I hear somebody shout my name in the coffee shop. I turn and look over in the corner by the front windows and recognize Brandon Stack, an old friend and baseball teammate from high school. I almost didn't recognize him. He's wearing a suit, the complete opposite attire of the usual mesh shorts and t-shirts that epitomize the fashion style of a typical college athlete. I walk over to meet him and he stands up and reaches out his hand and we slap palms before we shake.

"Dude, what are you doing in town?" Brandon asks me. "Shouldn't you be in New Mexico playing ball?" The last time we talked was a few years ago, when Brandon helped me train to get back in shape to play college baseball. We fell out of touch when I went away to school.

"I'm heading back soon," I say. "What are you doing here?" I figured he'd be playing professionally by now. He was MVP of our high school state-winning baseball team and had a full-ride to play in college.

"Just hanging out," he says. I notice that he's put on some weight in his face and his stomach. He doesn't have the typical summer tan we all get from playing over a hundred games under the sun.

"You're not playing baseball," I say.

"No, man, I had two shoulder surgeries last year."

Oh, shit. "Are you red shirting?" I ask.

He shrugs and shakes his head. "I've had too many injuries. I was ineligible the last two years for dislocated shoulders, sprains, you name it. I think I'm officially banned from the majors. I have the injury curse." He laughs but it's forced and there's an uncomfortable silence that starts to settle. How am I supposed to respond to that? *Hey, sorry to hear all your lifelong dreams will never come true. That really sucks.*

"So, you're finishing school?" I ask.

"Nah, my dad started up a real estate company a few years ago, so I joined him. I'm making a ton of money," he beams. "Probably just as much as I would have made in the pros. And I don't have to deal with all the physical abuse. I definitely prefer this career."

The dull glaze in his eyes contradicts his words. I can see a frustrated edge, when you realize life doesn't hand you anything, that you just need to enjoy every moment of success when you have it because everything is temporary.

"Good for you," I tell him because I think that's what he needs to hear.

"Besides, there's more to life than baseball. Right?" He laughs again. "I remember that girl you were with a few years ago, on Mill Ave? She said that to me. I thought it was the most ridiculous thing a person could say."

A strange déjà vu comes over me. I remember that day. It was the first time I had ever hung out with Dylan. I remember being so envious of Brandon when we ran into him on Mill Ave, wishing we could trade lives, jealous at everything he had compared to everything I had lost. I even remember being embarrassed to be seen with Dylan, like you're embarrassed to run into someone when you're in your pajamas, or tired or hung-over— when you're not at your best. What I hadn't realized yet was that when I'm with Dylan, I *am* at my best.

"I remember," I say. "Whatever happened to that girl you were with?" I ask him, remembering the supermodel he had glued to his side that day.

"What girl?" he asks.

I smile. He forgot about the girl he was *dating* and yet he still remembers something Dylan said. "Never mind," I say.

"What are you up to?" he asks me. I open my mouth and I'm about to rattle off that I signed with the Dodgers and my dad and I are going car shopping with my bonus check. But I remember why Dylan said those words to Brandon on Mill Ave. She always roots for the underdog. She said something ridiculous because she was supporting me, lifting me up, making sure I could walk away with my head held high. Maybe I need to pass the karma along.

"I'm just spending the day with my dad," I decide to tell him.

"Great!" he says, his eyes light. "Hey, if you're ever looking for a house in Phoenix, I can hook you up." He hands me his card with a well-executed draw and follows up with a savvy, salesperson smile. I wonder if he practices the fake smile in front of the mirror. It slips out as easily as his business card.

I take the card and slide my sunglasses down, over my eyes, before I put it in my pocket.

"Good to see you, Brandon," I say.

He walks back to his table and sits behind a laptop.

I turn and meet my dad and he hands me an iced coffee and we walk outside into the hot, dry air. I don't feel better than Brandon, or smarter or even luckier. I just feel like we are shaped so much by the events in our lives, but even more than that, we're shaped by the people that come in and out of our lives. I don't necessarily hope good *things* happen to Brandon. I hope a good *person* happens to him. I hope he's smart enough to realize it when it does. And to hold on.

Be sure to check out the other companion books in the Gray and Dylan saga, FIRST COMES LOVE and SECOND CHANCE. To find out more about Katie Kacvinsky and her books, check out her author website:

www.katiekacvinskybooks.wordpress.com